Hugo's Child

Susan M Higgins

SUSAN M HIGGINS

HUGO'S CHILD

An Amazon paperback

First published in August 2020

ISBN number - 9798638611682

Volume 3 in a trilogy

Copyright© S M Higgins

All right reserved. No part of this publication is to be published without the prior consent of the owner

All illustrations and Cover Design are copyright© by Heather Amelia Liptrott

Poetry Copyright© S M Higgins

Disclaimer

Hugo's Child is a work of fiction. Whilst places and areas are factual, the characters, incidents and dialogue within this book are purely fictional and are the products of the author's imagination. Resemblances to individuals or events are coincidental and are not to be construed as real.

SUSAN M HIGGINS

Books by the same author

Volume 1

Volume 2

SUSAN M HIGGINS

AUTHOR'S NOTE

Do we attach equal values to all human beings?

Is it right that some humans are considered to be less equal?

In an attempt to force autists* and individuals with learning differences to conform with neurotypical* norms, is society's rigid expectation of 'normal' biased?

Conversely, do neurodiverse* individuals expect those neurotypicals to comply with their own norms?

This thought-provoking work of fiction, challenges the myth of 'normal' expectations. Sharing their own paths, it focuses on a family whose intermingling blend of expectations, reveal their strive to accept and respect difference and uniqueness.

I invite you to read, absorb and digest its contents.

Autism is a lifelong neurodevelopment condition where the brain develops differently. It affects how a person relates to and communicates with others.

*An individual who has autism - a natural human variation - behaves in a manner which is considered to be 'abnormal' or 'different' by the general population. They are labelled as being 'neurodiverse'.

*A 'neurotypical' individual is someone who behaves in a way which is considered to be 'normal' by the general population.

SUSAN M HIGGINS

Nico's Wish

I see the world differently from you
I am different. You are different too

You do not understand me
I do not understand you

I misunderstand your behaviour, your words
You label me

You think I am disruptive and impolite
You become annoyed

You disregard me, exclude me
You do not try to accept me

Am I any less equal than you?

I do not need social acceptance from you
Neither will I disguise my autism for you

It is part of who I am

My autism is my advantage
Not my detriment

My wish is for understanding and
Equal values for all human beings

Can we all just learn to accept our differences?

SUSAN M HIGGINS

Sarah's Thoughts on Normality

My husband thinks
I adhere to needless societal expectations
He thinks I'm enigmatic

My son thinks
I'm always trying to change him
He thinks, that I think, I know what's right for him

I think
It's perfectly natural for me to
Think the way I do

We each think
Our ways are normal, but
I'm aware that my normal is not their normal

They are autistic
I'm not
We are different

I try to understand them
They try to understand me
We try together; it's difficult

I think, in time, my normal may become their normal
They think, in time, their normal can be my normal
We think, in time, our joint normal will be *'normal'*

We hope so!
Together
We're working on it!

SUSAN M HIGGINS

PROLOGUE

He, a young autistic child, is considered to be a musical genius and extremely precocious. With the support of his family, his key aim is to change the expectations and imbalanced perceptions of society in the Languedoc region of France, where he lives.

****

He, a high-functioning autist, a teacher, a husband and a father, uses his experience to facilitate change. When an unexpected letter from his birth father arrives, he finally forgives him for his abandonment.

****

She, a neurotypical, is married to an autistic man and is a mother to their autistic child. Whilst following her own vulnerable path, her life is enriched by her trials.

****

She, a spiritually informed educator, uses her previous experience to encourage individual enablement. When heartbreak unexpectedly visits her, she receives several clarifications, all revealing a confirmed link between her intuition and her past lives.

****

He, an acclaimed sculptor, nurtures his grandson and guides him as he strives to understand societal norms. When confronting a life-altering situation, he interprets purposeful meaning out of the pre-determined events which had occurred in his life.

CHAPTER ONE
June 2017

It was Nico's fifth birthday. He looked at the clock; 6.00am precisely. He always woke up at that time. The sun was just rising in the sky.

Later in the afternoon, after he'd attended his pre-school, he'd host a birthday party. Only one school friend, Enzo, would be coming.

Reluctantly, he'd been attending the Ecole Maternelle School in Lezignan for four half-days since he was three years old.

Even though, in France, the compulsory age for children to commence school was six, his mother had wanted him to socialise with other children. Recently, she'd heard on the news that the new president was soon going to make it compulsory for children to attend school at the age of three; in his effort to reduce inequality in education. She'd wondered whether the new education law would bring about some resistance.

During several discussions with other mothers, she'd learnt that whilst they wanted their children to have some form of pre-schooling, they also sought to nurture a close relationship with them before they went to school on a full-time basis.

Nico didn't like going to school. It wasn't that he didn't like learning; he did! He loved to learn about many things, but he knew he was different from the others. They didn't want to play with him.

They called him names. He just didn't 'fit in'. When he disputed the teacher's instructions, they dismissed his reasoning; labelling him 'disruptive'.

Reading was merely one of his numerous compulsions. His distinct bookishness had led him to acquire many fictional and non-fictional books, which he kept in librarian-order in a large bookcase in the corner of his bedroom. His writing skills had been compared with those of an eleven year old and his mathematical skills were excellent.

Articulate in both French and English, with an extended vocabulary for his age, he'd spoken in short, coherent sentences when he was just eight months old.

His father was French by birth and his mother was of English descent. Although his mother had a northern accent, when Nico spoke in English, his accent was formal and somewhat pedantic. His linguistic oddity became the topic of conversation when people met him for the first time.

Nico didn't particularly like being with children of his own age. He much preferred the company of his adult relations and friends.

At the grand age of three, he'd been placed in front of a piano and had stunned his parents and grandparents with his ability to play. Since being a baby, he had been exposed to all genres of music, especially classical concertos. With encouragement from his grandfather, who had initially spotted his innate passion for music and song, he'd learnt to replicate some of the famous classical composers. He would be placed on a tall stool at the piano and he would repeatedly practice the notes, until he'd perfected the complicated melodies.

When singing songs, he was word-perfect; his rote memory being excellent. If others sang the words incorrectly, he'd soon correct them.

For most of the time, the little boy was happy with his own company; especially when acquiring knowledge about a range of, what would appear to others to be, monotonous subjects.

When concentrating, he wasn't appreciative of interruptions. Neither did he welcome any change to his daily routine. Comparable to other children of his age, he was inclined to have tantrums.

Bordering on genius, Nico was diagnosed as being a high-functioning autist. There was always the possibility that he'd be autistic.

The diagnosis had come as no surprise to his

father, who was also a high-functioning autist!

CHAPTER TWO
June

Nico was excited. It was nearly 4.30 and his party was due to start.

He'd been practicing his party-piece daily for the last three months and, whilst his parents did encourage him to practice, it wasn't an expectation that he played every day. It was his own choice. If he didn't practice, he would become irritable. He was going to perform two pieces of music from Children's Corner, a solo performance by Claude Debussy.

He'd asked his mother if he could wear a white shirt and a black bow-tie when he was performing. She'd obliged, by taking him into Narbonne and buying them for him.

Extra chairs had been placed in the living area

to accommodate the guests. Refreshments would be served later, outside on the kitchen-terrace.

Before he made his entrance, he rushed to his mother, wanting reassurance. Unlike some other autistic children, Nico had absolutely no difficulty with expressing his emotions. He was a lovable child.

"Maman, hold me tight and wish me well."

Holding him in her arms, she hugged him.

He liked the feeling of her skin. As he gently touched her cheeks and stroked her forearm, he immediately felt comforted and reassured.

Sarah had only recognised the signs of autism when her son was around eighteen months old. As a neurotypical and a first-time mother, initially she'd thought that his peculiar mannerisms were just part of his babyish character.

Hugo, his father, had recognised signs earlier; at around twelve months old. It was easier for him to identify Nico's traits; they were very similar to his own.

She released him from her arms and quickly straightened his bow-tie. Seeing her five year old boy standing in front of her, in his short trousers and formal attire, caused her to bite into her bottom lip; to quell the salty tears that were already misting her vision.

Her son was so much like his father in looks, with his black, curly hair and strong pointed nose. His chunky build was the same as Hugo's and he had the same upright stance.

It seemed as if he hadn't been a baby for long. He'd grown far too quickly for her own liking; with an intelligence that was way beyond his infantile age. It had been quite difficult for Sarah to accept his behavioural differences at first and, it still was!

Nico's recent display of affection revealed his child-like desires, but later when he played to his audience, he would expose a maturity that was inconceivable for a boy of his age.

"Go, son. Your guests are waiting for you."

"Yes, Maman. I am fully prepared to deliver my best performance", he proclaimed.

She watched him descend the staircase; so very proud of him. Standing in front of his guests, he formally addressed them.

"Ladies and Gentlemen, may I thank you all for accepting my invitation. I am pleased to be playing for you this afternoon, two pieces from Debussy's Children's Corner suite of music. The first one is Serenade of the Doll and the second piece will be Jimbo's Lullaby."

Unhurriedly, he walked towards the impressive piano. His proud parents had recently purchased the individually- designed model for him.

As he positioned himself on the stool, his tiny fingers manipulated the keys whilst his foot could barely reach the soft pedal of the piano, to keep it depressed during his recital. Nevertheless, he was pitch-perfect as he performed the light-hearted Allegretto and, when he'd finished his piece, he turned towards his audience to receive their genial applause.

He beamed as loud hand-claps and shouts of 'Bravo' echoed around the confines of the living room.

Nico gratefully bowed his head in appreciation and waited for silence before he commenced his second piece; an enchanting lullaby which Debussy had dedicated to a stuffed toy elephant, whose name was Jimbo.

His fingers stroked the keys and the soothing tone encouraged his attentive audience to visualise the imaginary toy being lulled into a deep slumber.

Following a further five minutes of playing, he finished his recital and climbed down from the piano stool.

Standing in front of his guests, he gave several exaggerated bows.

"Thank you for listening to my performance. I trust that you all enjoyed it."

To a bystander, the way in which he addressed his audience could easily have been misconstrued as being precocious, but his guests were wholly accepting of his differences and loudly applauded him.

Reverting back to his earlier child-like state, he ran towards his mother and father for reassurance; revealing the two sides of his Gemini birth sign. He had been so extremely confident a few moments earlier and now he desperately needed their seal of approval.

They both embraced him.

His mother congratulated him. "Well done, Nico."

Hugo reiterated her sentiments.

"Excellente performance, fils."

Satisfied that he'd pleased his parents and his audience, he hurried over to his friend Enzo and they went outside to play.

Including Hugo and Sarah, there were eight adults.

Suzette and Serge Couture were 'adoptive' grandparents to Nico.

Hugo's mother, Nicole, had died before he was born and they'd informally, adopted Hugo. Serge had become a father-figure to him, after his birth father had left him when he was nine years old to go and live in America.

Hugo's love for his adoptive parents was so profound that he legally changed his surname to Couture and had named his son, Nico Serge Couture. His child's first name was in dedication to his late mother.

Suzette was Sarah's aunt and Serge's second wife. Her first married had ended in divorce. His first wife, Francesca, had died from cancer.

Six years earlier, Sarah had come to stay with her aunt and uncle for a holiday. She'd fallen in love with Hugo almost instantly. After returning to England for a short period to sort out her affairs, against her mother's advice, she'd hurried back to France to live with him.

Almost ten months later, their precious child,

had entered the world.

Extremely proud of his grandson, Serge had taught him how to organise his own routine of practicing on the piano and how to set individual targets. He was such a willing learner; so much so that his persistent approach to his learning had been proved in the professionality of his earlier performance. He still found it difficult to believe that Nico was just five years old.

Gabriel and Eve Le-Tissier were loyal family friends of Suzette and Serge. They'd first met each other when they'd attended one of Suzette's self-development courses. The following year, they had a joint wedding celebration with Hugo and Sarah. Nico had been christened at the same time.

Simone Moreau was the headteacher of the school for autistic children where Hugo had initially been a volunteer, but now worked on a part-time basis. She'd been instrumental in persuading him to study for a teaching qualification. Her instinct had alerted her to the fact that he'd make a significant difference to the students' lives; On their first meeting, she'd immediately identified his unique potential and had been most approving of his innovative ideas.

On several occasions she'd tried to persuade him to work full-time, but he was adamant about his desire to pursue other things; namely spending valuable time with his family, developing and promoting an organic food enterprise and fighting the cause for autistic children to be recognised and accepted.

Gilbert Guerisseur was the family doctor for the Coutures. He'd cared for Hugo's mother when Parkinson's Disease had callously invaded her body and ended her life. He'd also played an important part in the diagnosis of Nico's autism.

Gilbert had developed a fondness for Hugo and Nico; having worked closely with them and a selective group of other autists, studying their behaviour and development over a period of years. The information he'd gathered had been analysed and used to inform the funders of an international research project about adults and children, who were deemed to be high functioning autists.

Discussing volcano eruptions, rock formation and precious stones, Nico and Enzo sat separately from the adults, under the shade of the fig trees. They didn't want any distractions.

Enzo was also high-functioning; hence his ability to effortlessly converse and blend with his friend on a compatible level.

CHAPTER THREE
June

Following an hour of tantrums, refusals to eat his breakfast and get dressed, she'd eventually managed to safely instal him inside the car.

On the route there, his mood had worsened when she'd taken a different route. Thankfully, her son had decided he'd have merely a half-blown meltdown. A full-blown meltdown would have resulted in her returning home

"Please don't kick off now, Nico."

His formal tone was a reprimand.

"Maman, I must inform you that I am not kicking off anything. You know that we do not go this way to school."

"I know. I'm very sorry, but the roads are closed off in the village because there are workmen there. If I don't go this way, you're going to be late for school."

As she looked through her wing mirror, she could see him grinding his teeth and clenching his fists. She hoped that he didn't decide to undo his safety belt.

"I would prefer not to go, anyhow."

Frazzled, she drove through the side streets and arrived at school on time, thankful that it would soon be the summer holidays.

On their arrival at school, after trying to diffuse yet another tantrum, she was appreciative when one of the teachers finally persuaded him to go inside.

On reaching home, she exhaled a heavy sigh as she opened the door.

With a large mug of hot chocolate and a freshly-baked pain au chocolat, she lay back in the garden recliner at the side of a sculpture depicting a mother and child. Hugo, with the help of Serge who was a renowned sculptor, had created it in remembrance of his beloved mother. The gentle breeze wafted a myriad of aromatic fragrances from the wildflower garden. Her earlier angst was beginning to ease; but only a little.

She thought of how her life had transpired since she'd met Hugo. It was as if she'd entered another world; a novel world, which was far more interesting and challenging than the previous one she'd lived in.

Her mother had tried to dissuade her from

being with him, saying that his autism would be problematic. She'd been right in her neurotypical assumption.

When she had eventually heard of Sarah's pregnancy, she predicted that the baby would be autistic. She was right about that too.

However, what wasn't acceptable to Sarah, was the fact that her mother had only visited them a handful of times since Nico had been born. She'd had little contact with her grandson and he didn't really ask about his grandmother in England. He'd telephone and thank her for his cards and gifts at Christmas and on his birthday, but other than that, he didn't mention her name.

Her relationship with Hugo, although a very loving one, had intermittently been fraught with unexpected difficulties. Her husband was routine-oriented; she was flexible. He was literal; she was figurative.

His structured approach had been beneficial when she'd been recovering from giving birth. He'd organised everything to do with caring for the baby, wanting to make his wife happy and give her some time to recuperate, especially whilst she was breastfeeding.

He'd made sure that he'd bonded with Nico instantly after his birth. It was crucial for him. Sarah had also encouraged it, considering it to be an important part of his own healing. He was determined to give his son a different childhood to the one he'd had and he'd make sure that he'd be around to do things with him and teach him many things about life.

That was the main reason he only worked part time in the school. Hugo knew, from first-hand experience, the physical and mental anguish that rejection brings and, although he knew that his son would experience many forms of rejection in his life, he wanted to prepare him for it in a way which Nico would understand.

She smiled as she recalled the many times he'd tried to get her to breastfeed the baby, when the baby didn't want feeding. He thought that she should feed him at a specified time and that he should go to sleep at a precise time. His inflexible approach didn't work then; the baby fed from her when he was hungry.

Later on, his fixation on routines proved to be a blessing. The baby was put to bed at a certain time and a routine was established early on his life. That routine remained to this day. Her child's life was lived by routine; although there were times when he'd been poorly and the routine had been disrupted. That was when his illness had seemed twice as bad as it really was. At that time, she hadn't grasped that he'd inherited most of Hugo's traits. Just by being out of sync with his scheduled pattern, had confused him and made him irritable.

Hugo, Sarah and Nico lived by implementing codes and adhering to them; as much as they possibly could. Her expectations were different to those of Hugo and Nico. She had to explain to him that her ways were important to her and that whilst she was willing to bend to his habits, he also had to be prepared to make some changes and reach a compromise for their relationship to work.

He had forced himself to make adjustments. It wasn't an easy task. He loved her and wanted to please her. He'd had to make social changes too, in order to achieve academic success and later, when motivating his students.

On certain occasions, Hugo would display neuro-typical behaviour. On other days, his autistic traits would be at the forefront of his pursuits. He'd hyperfocus on mastering something to the nth degree for prolonged periods of time. Even though Sarah had read that hyperfocusing makes autistic people excellent achievers and experts in specific areas, it was a type of obsessiveness that she found hard to get used to.

On one occasion, she'd wanted some help and had hinted, instead of being direct. Hugo had thought that she was happy to do the job on her own. She was irked by his indifference to her unspoken request for help.

He'd reacted by saying "Why didn't you tell me that you wanted help? How do I know if you don't ask me? I can't read your mind or your body language – remember?"

She'd then remembered that she hadn't used their code of communication and she'd apologised for being so inconsiderate. How could she have expected him to have read her cues? Trying to decipher her moods or her mannerisms was not part of his make-up; although he was becoming more adept at 'reading her'.

Nevertheless, Hugo was starting to enjoy the guessing game. He was delighted when he had guessed accurately, especially when moments of intimacy were being proposed.

Whilst respecting his need to discuss his ideologies and potential ventures, she'd had to set time limits on his fixations during their discussions. Her sanity had been challenged on many occasions. There were only so many times she could endure hearing about the microscopic details of something which she had no interest in whatsoever; or didn't even understand.

When Nico had joined in the discussion, the intensity of it all had made her question the level of her own intellect. She'd left them to it.

One morning, when Sarah had called in at school to take Hugo his lunch that he'd forgotten, Madame Moreau had eagerly directed her to his classroom. Discreetly, she'd watched him for a while through the open door, witnessing the calm manner in which her husband adeptly reached his students; some of whom were very challenging to say the least. She was in awe of his limitless endurance and his altruistic approach towards their differences and disabilities.

She also remembered when Suzette had told her how he'd tenderly nursed his mother throughout her debilitating illness and how he'd done almost everything in his power to make her comfortable before she died.

This was her Hugo. The man that she loved with a passion. The unfathomable Hugo that was a sensitive, caring soul with a mission. *Her* husband.

She wiped the wetness from her cheeks with the back of her hand.

Her private time of reflection had given her a further appreciation of how blessed she was to have them both. They were the most important people in her life and her priority.

Taking shelter from the late morning sun, she picked up her plate and her mug and went back into the house. She had chores to do.

As she placed the dishes into the sink, she noticed a folded note on the worktop.

> Dear Maman,
>
> I would like to thank you for my birthday party.
>
> It was a very successful day.
>
> Nico x

Smiling, she re-folded the note. Reaching for her pen, she wrote the date in the corner. This note would go into her memories box with the other treasured notes which he'd written for her.

CHAPTER FOUR
June

Nico saw her again. It was the serene lady whom he'd dreamt about and had seen in his bedroom before going to sleep.

She was standing at the side of the statue, smiling at him.

He closed his eyes for a moment and then opened them again. She was still there.

Looking away, he carried on with tending to his small herb garden, gently smoothing the soil around the newly-planted seedlings. Since he had taken a great interest in gardening, his mother had allocated him a plot of his own to grow some herbs. Serge, taking his grandfather role very seriously, had assisted Nico in choosing some rosemary, lemon thyme, sage, basil and parsley to plant in his allotted area. Teaching his grandson about nature, art and life, was something he valued.

Curious, he stopped what he was doing and looked over towards the statue. The lady was still there, but the outline was now blurry. He blinked as she faded into the atmosphere.

He'd decided, that when he saw her again, he was going to say something to her and see if she answered him.

"Nico. Would you like a drink? It's hot out here."

"Oui Maman. Je voudrais de l'eau s'il vous plaît."

She was proud of the way in which her son would flip in and out of languages with a certain ease, speaking English and French simultaneously.

Sarah brought two glasses of iced water and sat down beside him.

"How was school this morning?"

"Maman, I *have* told you on many occasions that I do not like going to that school. The children do not want to play with me. I do want to play with them, but they do not play the game the way it should be played. I have told them that they have to follow the rules, but they run from me and call me names. I just play on my own, or with Enzo."

She was disturbed. The school had made her aware of her son's wilful behaviour; which they considered to be socially unacceptable. She was also aware that he hadn't been invited to the other children's birthday parties. Presuming that his idiosyncrasies were the issue, she felt angry.

Nico's interpretation of his own conduct was different to that of his teachers and the other children. He felt that he was being intimidated and that they were wrong in their misinterpretation of how he behaved and presented himself.

He sat close to his mother, snuggled into her and stroked her forearm. He could feel the warmth of her body and the smell of her perfume soothed him.

Holding him tightly, she wanted to protect him from all that was to come in his life, but she knew that she could only shield him so much; he'd have to work through his own struggles and learn from them.

From a neurotypical's point of view, how could she begin to understand how Nico thought or how he felt? Her parenting technique was different to Hugo's technique. It would be! She was so glad that he was autistic too. He would guide his son.

"Maman, can I ask you something?"

"Yes, darling. What would you like to ask me?"

"I sometimes see a lady standing by the side of Père's statue. I have seen her in my bedroom too, before I go to sleep. I have even dreamt about her."

Sarah smiled.

"Are you frightened?"

Staring directly into her eyes, he wriggled out

of her arms.

"No. I am not frightened. Why should I be frightened?"

She shook her head. He never ceased to amaze her.

"You shouldn't be."

"Do you believe me, Maman?"

He moved back towards her, wanting her reassurance that he wasn't telling lies.

"Yes, son. I believe you. Why don't you tell your père when he comes home from work?"

Unsurprised by what he'd seen or said, she'd also detected a spiritual presence several times. Having died a month before she'd met Hugo, Sarah had never met Nicole, but she knew everything about her. Her husband had made sure of that!

His mother had been a selfless woman, who'd devoted her life to her son; even when she was ill.

"I will."

Lifting his thumb in acknowledgement, he'd often wondered whether the lady was his Grand-mère Nicole.

Although he'd seen her on several occasions, he hadn't mentioned his secret to anyone before.
It was obvious that she still played an important part in their lives. The act of dying hadn't prevented her from having some influence over her grandson's life; nor her son and daughter- in-law's lives. She'd live amongst them, in spirit, for as long as was necessary.

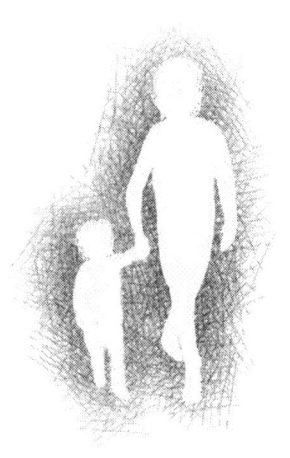

CHAPTER FIVE
July

Nico was lying on top of his bed. He went up to his bedroom at the same time each night. Routine was very important for his well-being. He would read his books or sketch some images of random objects. At other times, he'd just lay there pondering; staring into space or waiting for the lady to reappear.

Hugo and Sarah were sat outside on the terrace, drinking some home-made elderflower juice which he'd had made from the flowers in the garden. When he was a young boy, he'd helped his mother in her garden and she'd taught him how to make cordial. They'd gather the flower heads, severing the stalks carefully with sharp scissors. He recalled her instructions.

'Hugo, you must keep the flowers in an upright position. We don't want to lose the pollen. That's what gives the elderflower cordial it's unique taste.'

He'd trimmed the stalks and placed them on the compost heap. Then he'd gently placed the pink-tinged flowers into a bag until they were ready to be made into juice.

After washing the elderflowers, he'd put sugar and honey into a large pan with one litre of water and boiled it until the sugar had dissolved. Then he'd carefully submerged the elderflowers, some lemon juice and grated lemon zest into the liquid, leaving it to infuse for one whole day.

He never could wait for it to be ready. He loved straining the cordial through a muslin cloth and placing it into sterilised bottles. He felt as if he was operating his own little factory, manufacturing elderflower juice.

His mother had allowed him to have a little Limoux wine in his juice sometimes. Mostly, he'd just add ice-cold water to it.

Nearly everything he did, especially in the garden, reminded him of her.

He glanced at the statue and nodded.

"When I drink this juice, it always reminds me of her."

He raised his glass towards the statue, as if he was toasting her spirit.

Sarah already knew about the elderflower procedure. He'd described it several times.

Nodding her head, she smiled and raised her eyebrows. She allowed him his moment again. Even though they'd been together for almost six years, he still missed the signals. He accepted that raising her eyebrows was just something that she did.

"Hugo. I think we should consider whether we continue sending Nico to the nursery. He doesn't like it. I know he's only five and we said we wanted him to integrate with other children, but he's finding it challenging. I just want him to be a happy child."

Also concerned, he sighed as she continued.

"The teachers and the children don't really understand his repetitive mannerisms. There's too much sensory and social over-stimulation going on in the school. When someone sits in his chair or touches his belongings, he has a serious meltdown. They don't understand his inflexible adherence to the school rules and he believes that it is they who have unnecessary expectations."

When Hugo read bedtime stories to Nico, he could see the sadness emitting from his eyes when his son spoke about how the other children behaved towards him. Ever present in everything he did, he recalled his mother's words.

'Don't ever pretend to be something that you're not, Hugo. Always be proud of who you are and don't ever doubt your own worth. You are good enough, just as you are.'

Whenever he lacked in self-confidence she was

there with words of wisdom for him; always there to allay his fears.

'Be true to yourself. Don't ever judge yourself; there are plenty of others who will do that for you. Don't act out of character just to please others, whilst neglecting your own needs.'

He knew her words were relevant. He'd lost count of the numerous times he'd tried to fit in, aiming to satisfy others' demands.

Fully understanding of Sarah's concerns, his paternal instincts were in conflict with his previous experiences. Whilst he wanted to shield him, he also knew that Nico would need to mix with others to learn about life.

On the other hand, neither did he want his son to have to wear a social mask, like he'd tried to do when he was younger; struggling to live up to societal expectations. It annoyed him that the urge for some people to want to normalise others, was stronger than their unbending inability to accept that some people are just naturally different.

He'd spent several evenings analysing the long-term issues that his son would face and his own concerns overwhelmed him.

Recalling his own schooldays, he shuddered at the many incidents that had caused him misery. He'd hated going, but he had to agree that he'd also learnt quite a lot from his schooling.

Nevertheless, he'd gained an unhealthy reputation within several neurotypical schooling environments for, supposedly, being extremely uncooperative and disruptive; daring to express his own views, which were considered to be abnormal in relation to theirs.

He took hold of her hand and squeezed it. He didn't want her to worry.

"I want him to be happy too. He's spoken to me about it. We could homeschool him if you want to. Suzette's already been working with him.

He absorbs everything she teaches him."

"But is it considered legal to homeschool in France?"

He nodded.

"It's perfectly legal. He's still young and he doesn't have to go to school until he's six."

"I know I was instrumental in sending him there, but I'm having second thoughts. I feel guilty for forcing him to attend, when it makes him so unhappy? Do you think we should take him out of that school?"

He shrugged his shoulders.

"He's with Enzo. They play well together. When we've discussed it before, you brought me around to your way of thinking, when you said it was vital that he mixes; if only to get him used to others' views."

"I know. I'm sorry. Sometimes I don't know if what I'm doing is the right thing for him."

"If we decide, later on, that he should be homeschooled, all we'd need to do is inform the Mairie. Then we'd be inspected by the school inspectorate and as long as we conform with and adopt their curriculum, everything should be ok. Suzette has already said she'll continue educating him. We know she has the background. Let's see what happens."

Hugo was aware that the new president had made a promise to provide funding for autistic children's education. He'd already spoken with his principal about applying for funding to open a unit within the school for younger autistic children and other children who had learning differences and disabilities. The school had previously achieved great success in terms of progressing students with high achievement levels. A proposal had been formulated, and funding had been applied for. The school were expecting to receive a reply by the end of the summer term. He'd been instructed not to discuss it with anyone, until they'd been formally informed of the decision. He'd dutifully obeyed the instruction and was hopeful!

He had found it very uncomfortable when he'd met with the funding officials to put forward the school's proposal. For him, shifting between the role of an autist and a neurotypical wasn't a straightforward task. Performing in an unnatural, manner had caused him stress and it had been demanding; but he knew that it was in his own interests and that of the school, to step outside his comfort zone and attempt to manage his social anxiety in formal situations. The formalities of the initial meeting had expended almost all of his energy and he was glad when it had ended.

"Ok, Hugo. It's just that I do worry about him."

"I know you do and we'll do all we can to make sure he's happy. We both know that he'll have to develop several coping strategies, so that he becomes more resilient. It's inevitable that he'll encounter some problems and experience some anxieties, but we'll be there to help him through those challenges."

Her son had already inherited several of her husband's mannerisms and characteristics. She knew that he'd gain even more as he got older.

"We will be. Shall we go inside now? The pesky mosquitoes are finding me tasty!"

Hugo grinned.

"I find you very appetising too, ma chérie."

Interpreting his signal, she knew a night of passion awaited her. During their time together, she'd taught him how to pleasure her and their intimacy had developed into lengthy, love-making sessions.

Already physically aroused, he quickly blew out the citronella candles and, placing his arm around her shoulder, he guided her inside the house and locked the door.

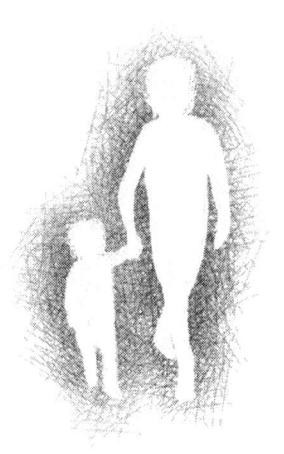

CHAPTER SIX
September

The first week of the new term had been hectic.

The Summer break had disrupted routines and his class weren't in the mood for learning, yet alone revising for their forthcoming exams.

He'd eased them back into their studies by having tutorials and allowing them to have extra study breaks during the day.

The eagerly-awaited letter from the funders had finally arrived.

Hugo had taken it from the postman at the school gate, before walking down the corridors to Madame Moreau's office.

Knocking on her door, he waited.

"Come in."

He handed her the letter.

"Well. Let's see if we've been successful."
Taking the letter knife from its stand, she carefully sliced the top of the envelope, before scanning its contents.

"Wonderful news. We've been accepted. We've got it. They've allowed us funding for the pilot project to be completed within two years and then, if we're successful, they say further funding will be reviewed."

The use of the school building was provided by the local council with the usual allocation of monetary funding; but extra support from parents and charitable donations enabled them to provide additional specialist equipment and resources to accommodate the different needs of the children.

This funding would allow them to breathe for a while.

They both grinned. The enormous task of writing the funding bid had been tiresome, but worth it. They were most grateful for the help they received from Gilbert Guerisseur, who'd spent many evenings with them both whilst they completed the obligatory and copious amounts of paperwork.

Gilbert had also spent several evenings alone with Simone. Following their initial meeting at Nico's birthday party, an irresistible curiosity had drawn him to her and, when the celebration had ended, he'd made sure he was in possession of her telephone number. Other than an obvious physical attraction, on both parts, there were many other commonalities. Both had a committed interest in developing children with learning differences and they shared the same quirky sense of humour.

Simone and Hugo felt certain that Gilbert's achieved acclaim for his keen involvement with the international, autism research project and his offer to volunteer his expertise, would have made an impression on the decision makers.

Hugo had also contributed by providing his own experiences of mainstream education. The school's existing record of achievement would have also been another deciding factor.

Gilbert had written a statement of integrity, outlining the successes of the school and the many benefits that the funding would bring; especially for those autistic children who found it difficult to function effectively within mainstream education.

"It's excellent news, Madame Moreau. We can now do so much more to help the children."

Throughout her teaching career, she had continuously cultivated an interest in educating children with different needs, focusing on solutions and not problems. Despite adverse conditions within the educational system, she had built her reputation on the fact that she provided a flexible, alternative curricula which suited the individual needs of those children who had, unfortunately, felt sidelined and unwelcome. The biased label of complex needs had been the mainstream school's justification for them not being deemed suitable for conventional education.

Even though there was an implied upward trend towards 'inclusion', the interpretation of the phrase was ambiguous. Some schools did not have the capacity to deliver and held low expectations of the children ever achieving.

Fully aware that some educationalists were against this form of 'segregated' learning, it was evident that there were still gaps in implementing inclusive education and, her diverse approach had made significant inroads into ensuring that those gaps were filled.

She wasn't advocating against inclusive education; far from it! What she was against, was the unnecessary phasing out of those educational establishments, who provided specific, meaningful education for those children with different needs.

"I must telephone Gilbert and tell him the good news. He'll be delighted."

Hugo left her to make the call and walked down the long corridor to his classroom to prepare for his lessons.

His head was spinning with ideas. If this project was successful, then perhaps more funding could be acquired to enable them to accept more children into the school.

His mission was to alter the cultural belief in France, that autistic individuals are damaged, dysfunctional and less equal than neurotypical people. The recognition of autistic people, their rightful place in society and the absolute right to be accepted for their differences was something that he wanted to make people aware of. He had other ideas which he'd also wanted to put into place outside of school; ideas which would challenge those neurotypicals in society who had their own misconceptions about autism. Those people who wanted to try to regulate how autists should live.

His own extensive research, as a teenager and latterly as an adult, had enlightened him to the fact that an autistic brain develops in different ways to a neurotypical brain. He'd read about how some doctors and scientists were looking for a cure for autism. He'd wondered if those professionals had ever considered whether autists wanted to be 'cured'; when they insensitively wrote their articles about autistic people, as if they had a disease or an illness. Had they ever contemplated that autists may be happy with the way they are?

He'd also read about a mainstream school in the north of France, which had achieved relative success by adopting inclusive teaching methods and by employing support workers to work with autistic children. He wondered how many of those workers had received the relevant training.

Idly glancing at his watch, he continued with his rumination.

Why do neurotypicals feel the need to fix things? Why can't they just accept that all human brains have areas which are both under and over-developed? Those neurobiological differences are what makes every human, unique!

The classroom was empty. The students

wouldn't arrive for another thirty minutes. He flicked through the funding papers. He'd need to study the terms and conditions thoroughly, before any concrete plans could be put into place. They'd applied to take in children from the ages of five and upwards, to eleven years; those children for whom mainstream was not considered to be suitable.

Whilst he did appreciate that, for some autists, mainstream education does work, he was certain that this innovative approach to schooling would assist the children in becoming more self-fulfilled and happier.

The majority of his extensive research had indicated that those mainstream schools who do accept autists, expect the children to integrate and adapt to neurotypical ways; with little or no adaptations being created to facilitate their needs. Specialist tutors were predominantly non-existent.

He was interrupted from his philosophies by a group of young boys who entered the room.

"Bonjour, Monsieur Couture", they shouted in unison.

"Bonjour les jeunes hommes."

They were a lively bunch, quite confident in their safe surroundings. They'd been problematic when Hugo had first arrived at the school, but they were now hard-working and very respectful of him and the position he held. Most of them were functioning at a high level and taking formal exams in the coming months; whilst others were working towards vocational qualifications.

"We'll wait for the others to arrive and then we can start. Thank you for being early for class."

Once the others had arrived, Hugo decided to open up a discussion about the word 'normal'; eliciting information from them on their opinions.

"It's only a word", was one answer.

"It's just an ordinary word that is used as a measure of expectation of human behaviour and responses", another student commented.

A less-confident girl, who was sat at the back of the group, plucked up courage and stated her view.

"This 'normal' thing is just a myth. Some people don't think we are normal. They think we are abnormal. They use words such as impairment, disabled, handicapped, and deficient. I don't like those words. They're hurtful."

Raucous cheers of agreement echoed inside the room. They were surprised at her contribution, considering she was usually somewhat reserved in her approach to discussions.

Another girl asked for quiet whilst she had her say.

"Monsieur Couture. I have a question for you. Why is it that some people think that autists need normalising? In our 'autistic eyes', we think that we are perfectly normal. Just because our normal isn't the same as their normal, they think that they are right and we are wrong. Well, we are not wrong!"

Her viewpoint resonated with his earlier

thoughts. The discussion was heating up and she continued.

"Some people also think that we prefer to be alone and that we are being anti-social. Ok, I do like to be alone sometimes, but I also have a social need when I like to mix with others. Does that make me abnormal?"

"Thanks for your pertinent question and your comments, Cecile. It's a very valid argument. Instead of using the word 'normal' we should aim to embed the notable word 'difference' into our vocabulary. Everyone in this room is different and everyone in this room should be proud of their differences and their identity. All neurotypicals are different too, but some fail to see that they are. Maybe they should take a closer look at themselves and analyse their own differences, instead of trying to dissect ours. We should be able to live our own normality."

Silence took its rightful place in the group, providing them with a stimulus for reflection. They looked at each other and nodded. Some smiled. Cecile was crying and a young man rushed over to comfort her. A positive awakening had occurred within her and the rest of the group.

Hugo continued with his theory.

"If any of you choose to believe that you are abnormal, impaired or any other of the negative descriptions that are used to stigmatise you, then you will become that person. Rise above it. You either stick up for yourselves or, if you don't, you are allowing them to continue to label you. It's up to you to do something about it."

His blunt words had produced a subdued effect. The room, once again, was silent; extreme shock settling on their faces.

Cecile's confidence returned.

"How can we stick up for ourselves when there's such a negative, cruel society out there, just waiting to exclude us and humiliate us?"

Hugo responded.

"You must remember that our autism does not define us. It's part of who we are and, whilst it is beneficial for us to be aware of neurotypical ambiguities and attitudes, it isn't necessary for us to conform to their subjective expectations. Some neurotypicals need to modify their attitudes and deviate towards accepting that we are all human beings and that we are just as equal to them. I'll let you think about what we've discussed and we'll continue with this discussion in another lesson. Take a break now. Go and have your lunch."

He pondered over what had been said. In his efforts to instil confidence into his students, was he trying to change them? Was he trying to encourage them to adopt neurotypical behaviour, so that they could 'fit in'? It wasn't his intention to turn them into robots, where they did things that were unnatural to them, just to be accepted!

Living with a neurotypical and mixing with neurotypicals, he'd sometimes questioned whether some aspects of autism resided in the behaviour and minds of *all* humans. If he chose to sensitively analyse the habits of humans, he'd undoubtedly discover numerous idiosyncrasies.

Another contentious issue floated inside his head, as he addressed the empty room.

"Anyhow, who decides what's right for one person and what's not right for another? How *is* an autist supposed to act and react?"

He opened his lunch-box and a note from his son sat, neatly folded, on top of his baguette. Unfolding it, the neatly written words made him smile.

> Mon Père
>
> Je vous souhaite une
> bonne journée de travail.
>
> Nico x

It was another surprise note from his son, wishing him a happy day at work.

As he bit into the baguette, he felt certain that his lesson had given them all some 'food for thought'.

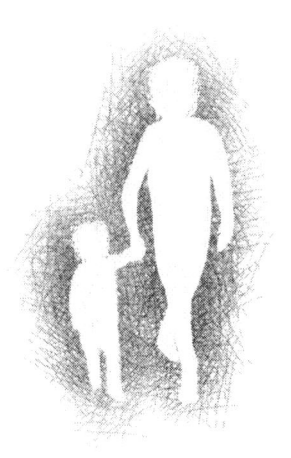

CHAPTER SEVEN
September

Hugo's life had been demanding of late. He was exhausted and his life felt disorganised.

Students had been anxious whilst revising for their autumn exams. Nico had wanted constant encouragement concerning his latest musical composition. Sarah had urgently needed his advice on things to do with the house and he was trying to prepare the necessary paperwork for the start-up of his organic food enterprise.

Not only was he developing a curriculum for the new unit within the school, he'd also been busy developing a pre-employment programme, with the help of Suzette, for those vocational students who wanted to work, rather than progress into higher education. They would take their exams early.

It was the school's main aim to support and encourage the older children to complete their education and progress into higher education or employment.

Built into the programme were interview techniques, role-plays, CV writing, communication skills and social skills.

With the help of Serge, Hugo had contacted local employers to ask if his students could go into their businesses on work placements.

Whilst a few of them were more than happy to consider work placements, some quoted health and safety requirements as their excuse for not allowing the students on their premises. He knew it would be a tough task, but he'd pursued with his mission and, after making contact with a total of seventy employers, he'd managed to gain seven interviews; all friends and acquaintances of Serge!

As a volunteer advocate, Suzette had visited each employer beforehand, to provide background information on the project. She had also discussed the setting up of an employer networking group to address any issues; of which she and Hugo would be the main links.

One particular student, Pierre, had difficulty with making eye contact. He'd get angry if he was interrupted and then he'd refuse to speak. Hugo had spent a considerable amount of time with him, trying to build his confidence skills and was pleased to hear him voice his wish.

"I want to work, Monsieur Couture. I want a job. I want to contribute to society", he declared.

Trying to be as sensitive as he could, he answered him.

"That's good to hear, Pierre, but you'll need to work on improving your social skills before you go for interview."

Pierre averted his eyes and looked out of the window. He knew exactly what his teacher was inferring, but he wasn't a social person. He also knew that if he wanted to get a job, he'd have to make an effort.

"When you do go for interview, introduce yourself and thank the person for inviting you to be interviewed. Then, you must tell them how you present yourself. Tell them that you're autistic and that if you don't make eye contact during the interview, it's not that you are being impolite, it's just that it's part of who you are."

He didn't like the idea of telling anyone that he was autistic. He'd felt inferior when his parents had apologised for his directness, openly blaming his autism. When in conversation with others, they had disrespected his difference; assuming that he hadn't heard their negative comments. He'd heard every single word. Afterwards, the same people had treated him differently, as if they were feeling sorry for him. He'd hated it. He didn't want people to feel sorry for him. He wanted acceptance, not pity!

He'd also remembered how they'd thought he

was strange when he hyperfocused on his own interests. He felt like saying they were the strange ones with their absurd fixation with sport – even to the point of worshipping the football players and the game!

"I don't know if I can do that", he asserted.

"You could ask them if they'd allow you to finish answering one question, before they ask you another. Just explain to them that it interrupts your concentration."

"What if I'm asked lots of questions at once and I get angry?"

"That's what we'll work on, Pierre. You'll need to be mindful that most employers will not understand your autistic traits. However, you can be an ambassador, educating the neurotypicals in our society about autism. How will they ever learn, if *we* don't teach them?"

A smile crept onto Pierre's face and stayed there for a while. He wondered if he could do it. He wondered if he could get people to understand. Maybe, he'd give it a try!

"Another thing you need to consider is the fact that you may not be successful the first time, or even the second or third time, but there will be someone out there who will be willing to employ you."

Hugo had undertaken extensive research on the employability of autists, especially in England, where employers were further advanced in their knowledge and understanding.

He'd also been optimistic when Suzette had told him how some larger organisations in England and America had been astute enough to employ neurodiverse individuals. She'd claimed that they recognised and respected how some autists possessed excellent cognitive skills and how they were able to effortlessly scan volumes of data, analyse trends and make decisions; all of which were beneficial for the future of their businesses.

She'd further enlightened him of how the English government took the issue of social responsibilities seriously and how a recent strategy had been set up, to encourage the employment of people with learning differences and disabilities.

Hugo and Madame Moreau had already discussed the possibility of Suzette volunteering her skills for two half days per week and the necessary clearance had been obtained for her to commence working in the school. Her previous teaching experience of individuals with different needs would be invaluable.

He observed the rows of perplexed faces.

"We have to get out there and make our views known. However difficult it may be, we have to get the message across that we are all equal; no matter what others my think. We all deserve to have a rightful place in society."

Their teacher's odd suggestions were alien to them. They had become accustomed to being excluded and were frightened by the thought of moving forward in wider circles. They didn't know if they could do it!

"I do have some idea of what you may be thinking. You feel safer being with other autists or just being alone, or with people who understand you."

He sensed their fear. He'd also experienced the same fear when he'd first arrived at the school as a volunteer.

One student shouted out.

"I'm not going for an interview. How scary would that be?"

His rhetoric provoked an agitated discussion within the group and Hugo subtly encouraged the debate, by allowing it to continue.

Above the raised voices, Pierre managed to speak.

"Monsieur Couture, I'd like to try. I want to work. I think I could do it."

Impressed with Pierre's attitude, he secretly hoped the others would feel the same way. If they wanted to form and maintain social relationships, it would be good for them to have a work-oriented daily routine. If they didn't, well that was also ok. For those who did, there was the possibility of them achieving social status by working towards professional qualifications.

"I'm certain you can do it, Pierre"

Having regained their complete attention, he continued to explain how he would be delivering specific lessons to help those who wanted to be considered for interview.

Following further conversations, a total of seven students, including Pierre, were willing to go for an interview; thereby making up the quota for the seven already-discussed placements.

Suzette would pay further visits to the workplaces to arrange for interviews to take place.

Their transformation was both encouraging and conflicting for him. Whilst they'd all taken a massive step out of their comfort zones, he did consider whether his own actions may be forcing them to embrace neurotypical behaviours!

Being autistic and living in a neurotypical world was problematic!

CHAPTER EIGHT
September

Market day in Lezignan was always bustling. Sarah loved bargain-hunting and the friendly bartering with the stallholders. Most Wednesdays, after they'd been shopping, she and Suzette would call into a popular café at the far end of the main thoroughfare.

Heavily laden with several shopping bags, they pushed their way through the crowds and into the café. Sarah managed to locate two seats near the serving counter and quickly claimed them, by placing her bags on them.

"Come on Auntie Suze. Quickly. I've found two seats over here."

Not answering, she had been distracted by the sight of two people whom she'd been acquainted with seven years ago. They were sitting in their usual place by the side window. Several times, she'd imagined that there could be the possibility that she'd see them again. Living as she did, in close proximity to where they lived in Olvano and, paying regular visits to the market, she was surprised that she hadn't bumped into them sooner.

He'd spied her as soon as she'd entered and had willed her to look at him. She did. He held her gaze and half-smiled, not knowing how to react or how she'd react.

She pretended she hadn't seen him.

The woman, sat beside him, was aware of his inattentiveness and turned around to see who he was gaping at. Visibly shocked, her jaw dropped as she spotted Suzette. No half-smile from her. Her lips puckered as she rolled her eyes and leant over to whisper in his ear.

"Over here, Come on."

Squeezing through the crowded room, she sat down in the vacant seat. She really wanted to leave. Even with the air-conditioning blowing out cool air above her, she was hotter than she'd ever felt when she'd been out in the blazing sun.

Subconsciously, she repeatedly bombarded herself with questions.

"Why do I feel agitated? Why am I allowing them to take my energy? How *did* you think you'd feel when you saw them again? What happened, seven years ago, is in the past. I've forgiven them, so why do I feel so strange?"

The waiter hovered over them, prompting them for their order.

"Same as usual, Auntie Suze?"

She nodded, absently.

Sarah practiced her fractured French.

"Un Americano, un chocolat chaud très chaud et deux tranches de gâteau aux carottes, s'il vous plait."

Puzzled by the distracted expression on her aunt's face, she quizzed her.

"Don't you feel well? Is the heat getting to you?"

"I'm ok. I've just caught sight of two people who I knew a long time ago and I don't want them to come over and talk to me."

Suzette had noticed how suave he looked with his white linen shirt and his navy chino shorts. His spiky, gelled hair was much thinner and greyer than when she'd last encountered him. She noticed also how his piercing, electric-blue eyes had widened and glistened through his designer spectacles, as he'd hesitantly smiled at her.

The woman, who was sat close to him, was dressed impeccably in her Lagerfeld striped shirt and fitted jeans. She looked so much better than when she'd last seen her. Alcohol and too much sun had ruined her skin and her posture had been stooped, then.

She wondered if they were a 'couple' now. The woman had always worshipped him.

The waiter brought their drinks and two ample chunks of carrot cake.

"What's the matter? You look as if you've seen a ghost."

Laughing at her comment, she placed a forkful of cake into her mouth.

"Two ghosts", she replied.

Sarah shrugged her shoulders and raised her eyebrows.

"Are you serious?"

"I'm speaking metaphorically."

Sarah chuckled.

"Well, I can never tell with you. You're forever seeing people and things. Would it, by any chance, have something to do with those two people sat near the window in the corner?"

"Why do you say that?"

Taking a deep breath, she exhaled. She'd been watching them, watching her and Suzette. Sipping her coffee, she spoke from behind her cup.

"Well, if it is those two, he's coming over to our table, now."

Suzette stiffened. Her inner voice spoke.

"Be polite. Don't react. Remember, you've forgiven him; and her."

Practising what she preached, she relaxed. Her breathing slowed down and she willed herself to remain calm. She should be thanking them, not feeling angry towards them. They'd both been a necessary part of the arduous path which she'd been treading, on her journey to meeting Serge.

He tapped her on the shoulder, leaned in close and kissed her on both cheeks.

"Bonjour, Suzette. How wonderful to see you. It's been a long time."

She forced a smile. He was wearing the same cologne as he always wore.

"Bonjour, Jurgen. It *has* been a long time. How are you?"

He answered in his broken English.

"I'm so very fine, thank you and you?"

"Good, thanks."

Although, initially, it was a shock to see him, she knew that she felt no animosity towards him. She sensed that he was still a lost soul, trying to find his way back onto his own path.

Seeing the wedding ring on her finger, he subtly continued.

"You are here on holiday? Where are you staying?"

She shook her head.

"No, I'm not here on holiday. I live here."

His jaw dropped. He hadn't heard anything 'on the grapevine' about her returning to France; but then he wouldn't have! He'd returned to his other home in Germany soon after what had happened and, even though he'd tried to make contact with her several times, by letters and by endless telephone calls, he hadn't been successful. Foolishly, he'd let her slip through his fingers. It was too late, now!

"Oh! How wonderful for you. Where do you

live?"

Not wanting to lie to him, or even more so, to give him information on where she lived, she tactfully answered.

"On the outskirts of Lezignan."

Sensing that more questions would follow, she moved her foot and kicked Sarah's leg under the table.

Sarah stood up and gathered her bags.

His eyes rolled upwards as he scanned her lightly-tanned figure. He wondered if the young woman was English; she looked English. As soon as she'd walked into the café, he'd noticed her slim frame, her full breasts and her excellent pair of legs.

"Come on, Auntie Suze. We must go now. I promised Nico we wouldn't be late."

Thankful for the interruption, she picked up her own bags.

"Well, it was so nice to meet you again, Jurgen. Take care."

As he leant over to kiss her again, she could see the woman and Sarah watching them.

Jurgen whispered in her ear.

"You look very beautiful, Suzette. I'm very sorry for what happened."

She didn't flinch.

"There's nothing to be sorry for."

Surprised by her reply, he smiled. Had she forgiven him? Had she really forgotten what had happened? He'd subtly interrogate the villagers in

Olvano, to see if anyone had heard anything about her, or where she lived, or who she was married to. Someone would know. Everyone knew everything about everybody in this locality.

"Au revoir, Jurgen. Take care."

As she left the café, she casually waved at the woman in the corner and smiled.

"Au revoir, Valda."

Jurgen had frequently wondered if he'd see her again. Now he had!

CHAPTER NINE
September

On their journey home, they stopped off at the local patisserie to collect some bread and a tarte au citron. Suzette hadn't done any baking for several days. She'd been far too occupied in the orchard, harvesting ripe berries and fruits.

As soon as they got into the car, Sarah was inquisitive. She couldn't wait to find out who the man was.

"What was all that about? Who was he?"

She briefly relayed about how she'd met him a few years ago; how he'd wooed her, then tried to control her and how he'd deceived her.

"Oh! There was something about him that I couldn't explain. He's a bit of a charmer, isn't he? I just felt as if he was undressing me with those icy-blue eyes. He kept ogling me and grinning."

Suzette nodded. He hadn't changed one iota. A leopard never does change its spots!

"Yes. He's a charmer alright. He does have a 'thing' for the ladies, especially younger women. He's so adept at casting spells. He cast one on me and I fell for it; for a while anyhow! I soon realised his game and I walked away from him."

"Tell me, who was the woman that he was with?"

"She's a close friend of his. He manipulated her too. She was madly in love with him and I think she still is! When I started having a relationship with him, she was furious and became very cruel towards me."

Sarah scowled.

"There's more to it than that. He was also seeing another woman who lived in Perpignan. At the time I was angry, confused and very hurt. But I worked through it. It was meant to happen. I should be thanking them both and I already have; subconsciously, not literally. I wouldn't have met Serge if I'd still been with him. They were part of my path; as was the other woman. Although I've forgiven them, it was still a shock to see them. It seems like a different lifetime now."

"How can you forgive so easily?"

"Forgiving is healing, Sarah. I wasn't going to hold onto something negative that happened in the past. Neither was I going to let them have any power over my thoughts."

She nodded, admiring the assertive manner in which her aunt dealt with things; quite different to her own mother. Sarah hoped she could forgive her mum's lack of interest in her family.

Both preoccupied with the recent event, they continued strolling for a while, in silence.

"What are you thinking, Sarah?"

"I just wish Mum would telephone Nico from time to time. It's not how I wanted it to work out. I wanted her to have a presence in his life and be interested in my life also."

"The situation is what it is. You have to deal with it in your own way."

She knew she would; but still she couldn't help wishing it was different.

"Holding onto something which doesn't serve a purpose in your life is disempowering. Just do your best and learn as much as you can from the situation. You know, we can't always have what we want."

Jokingly, she answered.

"Ok. Here endeth the lesson!"

Before entering the patisserie, the two of them gazed longingly through the glass window.

Strawberry tartlets, tiny caneles, mendicants, macarons, mille-feuille and an assortment of petit fours were all immaculately arranged in organised symmetrical rows.

Suzette knew that once she'd entered the patisserie, she'd leave with several boxes of cakes for the afternoon tea gathering, which she'd earlier arranged. She had a sweet tooth, as did Serge; that was one of the reasons she baked most days. It would be a pleasant change to eat cakes and pastries which someone else had baked.

Sarah's saliva glands were stimulated every time she visited this bakery.

"Thanks for inviting us over later."

Suzette had also invited Eve and Gabriel. Her friends had enjoyed numerous escapades in several countries and she was excited to hear about their latest adventure.

They packed the cake boxes into the rear of the van and took a short cut home, through the country roads.

As she drove up the gravel path towards the house, she glimpsed her husband and her grandson on the kitchen terrace, making clay models.

"Look at them, Sarah. Nico loves being here with his grand-père. He's so happy when he's with him."

This was exactly what Serge had yearned for when he was younger; to care for his own child. Sadly, it was not to be. His first wife, Francesca, had miscarried several babies before she died. He was embracing every second of his grandson's life. Every chance that he had, he'd spend time with him. On the days when Hugo and Sarah were working and Nico wasn't in school, they'd devote their time to just being with him and enjoying his company.

They'd been cultivating his creative side ever

since he was a toddler; by ardently nurturing his excessive interest in music and art.

Serge was also focusing on improving Nico's social skills; although lately, it was proving to be problematic. He constantly liked to dominate the conversations. If interrupted, he'd become angry and anxious. Inevitably, a meltdown would follow.

In naturally occurring situations, especially when they were alone, Suzette had used applied reinforcement techniques to help with managing his inappropriate emotional eruptions. Together, they'd set a goal to work towards and, each time he'd succeeded in controlling his interruption and meltdown, he'd receive rewards; mostly books. It worked for him, although she did accept that it doesn't necessarily work for others.

He seemed to have gained much enjoyment from achieving, knowing that he'd pleased her just by obeying the rules.

She was conscious of the fact that some people would argue that she was trying to make him appear as if he wasn't autistic, by trying to change his behaviour. From her understanding, she wasn't. Nevertheless, they did have a point!

His parents were happy with Suzette using the technique and, instead of making him anxious, it had produced an adverse effect.

Recalling how he had easily mastered several development milestones at an early age, the sheer magnitude of his intelligence had astounded her. In recent conversations, he'd recall events that had occurred when he was two years old. He'd use new vocabulary and when she asked him how he knew that word, he distinctly informed her that he 'just knew'. He even gave her an explanation of the meaning of the word, in great detail.

At other times he'd appear vague; as if he wasn't listening and was having some trouble processing the information. She couldn't decide if he didn't understand or if he just wanted time to absorb the information and store it for later use.

Sarah was pleased with how her aunt was teaching her son to become more self-aware.

"Well, it looks like you two are having lots of fun there." She shouted.

Nico quickly covered his work with a cloth. Distracting him from what he was doing had irked him and his reply was harsh.

"We are Maman, but do you not know that it is impolite to interrupt. Grand-mère says so."

Suzette wanted to laugh but she refrained from doing so. He had taken her literally when she had been teaching him the rules.

Sarah also had to contain her laughter; she was used to his candour.

"Sorry. I'll try to remember for next time."

"It is just being polite, Maman. Once you have learnt the rules, you will be fine. Grandmère says so."

His imitation of his grandmère's voice was exact. He loved to duplicate what he'd heard.

Leaving them to continue with their work,

Suzette had discovered something else about her grandson.

"I'll have to be careful what I say in future. He has a habit of repeating what I say."

"He does it all the time with us. Sometimes I can't distinguish between him and Hugo. He uses the same tone of voice as him. I had to stop myself laughing then."

"Me too. He's so funny without realising it; although he wouldn't really understand why we were laughing, would he?"

Sarah couldn't answer. Her emotions were rising up from within her chest and grabbing her throat. The many adversities that her son would encounter throughout his lifetime, were only just beginning; but she'd remain positive and focus on his strengths and not his weaknesses.

CHAPTER TEN
September

Whilst Sarah and Suzette had been busy in the kitchen, Nico had been equally as engrossed in the completion of the clay sculpture for his mother. It was a gift for her and she'd nearly ruined the surprise!

Approximately 300mm in height, it was a miniature version of his père's creation and, when it had been fired in Serge's kiln, he'd present it to her.

Sarah carried the empty plates and napkins to the table, which was already groaning with the weight of an assortment of savoury and sweet food. Glancing over at her son, she noticed that Hugo had arrived home from work.

He waved at her and blew her a kiss.

He still had the ability to make her heart perform several front somersaults. As she lovingly pressed her fingers to her lips and returned a kiss, she was distracted by a car pulling up on the gravelled driveway.

It was Eve and Gabriel. They'd just come back from India, where they'd been volunteering their skills.

She walked over to the car and embraced them; eager to hear all about their travels.

The others rushed over to welcome them; except Nico, who was mindfully unaware.

At 4.15pm, all were seated around the table, with the exception of the little boy.

Sarah called her son to the table.

"Nico. Come and eat. We're all waiting for you."

His eating routine was being disrupted. It wasn't his time to eat. It was too early to eat! He pretended he hadn't heard her and continued to work on his creation.

"Nico", she shouted again.

He looked up and saw her approaching. Quickly, he covered his work and stomped angrily towards the table. He disliked being interrupted when he was concentrating and, anyhow, he wasn't hungry yet. Although he loved his maman, she wasn't like his père. She didn't understand him.

"Maman, why must I come to the table to eat?"

Agitated, he paced around the table several

times before his father took hold of his hand and directed him to his seat at the side of him.

Shaking his head, he sighed, shrugged his shoulders repeatedly and fiddled with his napkin.

Suzette handed him a plate of his favourite cheese sandwiches. The crusts had been removed, the cheese had been sliced thinly and they were cut into tiny triangles.

"I've made these especially for you, Nico. Just how you like them."

"Merci, Grandmère."

He pushed them around the plate before looking at his watch. He'd leave them for a while before he ate them.

Concerned about his fixation with specific types of food, Sarah tried to tempt him with a cheese scone.

"Try one of these. They're delicious."

Straightening his back, he clenched his fists and began arranging the serving plates in neat lines on the table. He was uncomfortable with how they were unevenly placed.

"Maman, why do you keep trying to make me eat the food which I do not like?"

"You won't know if you like it until you try it." Hugo nudged him.

Mumbling to himself, he bowed his head. He understood that his père thought that he was being impolite; although he didn't actually consider it to be impolite to state that he didn't want to eat food which he didn't like!

Already irritated, he became even more anxious when he saw the earrings.

"Maman. May I ask you something, please? Why are you still wearing those earrings?"

Before she'd left for the market earlier, he'd noticed the earrings then. Any small change in her appearance would trigger a tantrum. She'd been in a hurry and had forgotten to change them to the usual ones she wore.

Considering the impact of her forgetfulness, she stayed calm, removed the earrings and slipped them into her pocket. It was so much easier to remove them, than attempting to reason with him. Neither did she want to exacerbate the situation.

"Thank you, Maman."

For a few moments, they sat in silence.

Diffusing the awkwardness, Eve started to speak about their time in India.

"We've spent most of the last three months working in Nepal, assisting with the installation of water-purifying systems in several villages."

When Eve had lived in England, she'd been a sponsor of a charity who donated funds to help those people who didn't possess the privilege of drinking clean water on a daily basis.

"We also helped to raise awareness of the importance of hygiene practices and the benefits of good nutrition. I have to say that I was saddened to see how subservient some of the women were in the poorer villages. They simply accepted their existence and didn't complain. Although, we did see some younger women who were desperate to leave; not wanting to live the traditional way of life."

Suzette was dismayed also.

"I bet that was a shock for you, Eve?"

Eve nodded, recollecting her experiences.

"It certainly was. Superstition ruled in the villages and they believed that awful things would happen to them, if traditions weren't followed."

They all listened intently, including Nico, as Eve continued describing the appalling conditions and the desperate lives of the villagers.

"When working in a children's make-shift hospital, Gabriel's GP experience and specialism in the treatment of respiratory diseases, had been advantageous. Most of the babies and children had contracted diseases. They had severe breathing problems, through inadequate nutrition, lack of clean water and sanitation-related illnesses. It was so distressing to witness their misery."

Nico felt sad. The poor children who were living in India were drinking dirty water and didn't have much food to eat - and he'd grumbled about eating different food, which he hadn't attempted to taste.

Gabriel nodded in agreement with Eve.

"It was very painful to witness. Sometimes the children lost their will to live. They didn't have the energy to fight their illnesses. We didn't have the medication to treat some of those children who were severely ill. Change needs to happen and that change needs to happen quickly. Even though Eve and I had the necessary vaccinations before we went to India, we still contracted a milder attack of diarrhoea and we were quite ill for several days."

Suzette wiped her eyes with the back of her hand.

"Oh, Gabriel! It must have been awful to witness the children suffering so much."

"It was; very much so! We were working eighteen-hour days within the immunisation clinics and on overcrowded wards, where life-threatening illnesses were rife. Many vulnerable children had contracted cholera and their desperate mothers were begging us to heal their severely dehydrated children; some of whom also had pneumonia."

Nico got up from his chair and scrambled onto Sarah's knee. Snuggling into her, he wrapped his arms tightly around her.

Folding her arms around him, she laid his head on her chest. Rocking him, she whispered in his ear and kissed his head.

"It's ok, darling."

She felt guilty for allowing him to hear their conversation. Maybe she should have allowed him to stay at his crafting table, instead of insisting he joined them to eat.

"But it is not ok, is it Maman? We must do something to help those people. What can we do?

"We'll think of something, son."

The others watched in silence as the little boy wrestled from her grasp and stood in front of them. Whilst repeatedly humming several tunes and making sweeping hand movements, he looked as if he was conducting an orchestra. He then excitedly tapped his fingers on the table as if he was playing his piano.

"Maman, I could perform a piano recital like the one I did at my birthday party. We could ask people to pay some money to come and watch me play. I would do my very best for them. What do you think about the idea?"

Proud of him, she bent down and placed another kiss on the top of his head.

"I could also read some of my poems and Grandmère could bake some cakes. We could give all of the money we make to the poor children so that they can be well again. Would you say that was a good idea?"

Nico's compassionate offer of help had lifted their melancholic moods.

Hugo lifted his son and swung him around.

"It's a great idea. We'll make plans."

Suzette had sensed a significant change of mood in her dear friends. Not only had Eve and Gabriel lost weight, their wrinkled brows revealed traces of the traumatic events they'd witnessed. Being highly-sensitive individuals, it was patently obvious that their experiences had given them an elevated meaning to what it was like to be human.

Gazing fondly at the people sat around the table, she was so thankful for everything that was present in her life!

CHAPTER ELEVEN
October

Pierre woke up again. Having hardly slept, he was overly tired. Feeling nauseous about his interview, he was unable to eat his breakfast.

Hugo collected him at 8.45. They were only expected at 10.00, but he wanted to make sure that they were there with plenty of time to spare.

As the car pulled away from the house, his mother waved anxiously.

Aware of her concern, he forced a shaky smile and waved back.

The interview was to take place in a well-known restaurant in Narbonne, which belonged to one of Serge's closest friends, Gaston.

Having already discussed Hugo's project with him, Serge had briefed him on Pierre's interest in cooking. Happily, he'd agreed to be involved.

They left the car in the car park alongside la Robine Canal and strolled, in silence, along the tree-lined street which runs through the heart of Narbonne. Several small boats were moored to the side of the canal and the city centre was less crowded than it was on market days.

The heat of the morning sun was nothing compared to the heat that was emanating from Pierre's body. His white shirt revealed sweat stains under the arms and beads of sweat dripped down his forehead and into his eyes. It was already 19 degrees and the forecast predicted 28 degrees later in the day.

As they entered the restaurant, a concierge greeted them before escorting them to a private seating area.

Hugo watched as Pierre's body shuddered. The young man had placed his portfolio on his knees and was uncontrollably tapping his fingers around the edges.

He moved over and sat beside him.

"Pierre. Take some deep breaths and try to remember what we spoke about yesterday. Think only positive thoughts. Imagine yourself working in this restaurant."

"I have Monsieur Couture. I have been. I've been using the 'self-talk' technique ever since we did it yesterday. All morning, I've been trying to get rid of the internal muttering inside my head."

Captivated by the proximity and splendour of

his surroundings, his eyes surveyed the vivid paint daubed randomly onto three enormous, abstract paintings. Positioned against the stark backdrop of the pure white walls, they appeared, to him, to be images of people dining, but to others they may have just looked like geometric shapes.

"I'm not used to anything like this. It's very grand."

Hugo was apprehensive; also overwhelmed by the magnificence. Not wanting to transmit any discouraging energy onto Pierre, he focused all of his energy on remaining calm.

"It is a stunning venue, Pierre. Just try to do your best. I have every confidence in you."

"I will. I'll try."

Sidetracked from their conversation, they watched as a tall gentleman, dressed in traditional chef whites with a white bandana tied at the right side of his neck, strode energetically towards them. The man removed his *toque blanche* and placed the immaculately pleated hat on the table in front of them, before extending his hand to Pierre.

Pierre froze. He kept his hands by his side.

Hugo immediately reacted by reaching out for the man's hand and shook it firmly. Serge had taught him that a firm handshake indicated a sense of self-confidence.

"Bonjour Monsieur Lemaire. My name is Hugo Couture. This is Pierre Franco. Thank you for taking time out of your work to speak with us."

"Bonjour Hugo. Serge has spoken fondly of

you, many times."

Recognising the severity of Pierre's anxiety, Gaston invited them both to take a seat, before joining them. Wanting to alleviate Pierre's unease, he sat beside him, so that the interview wouldn't appear to be too formal.

Pierre fidgeted in his seat and moved away slightly. The close proximity had alarmed him.

Hugo relaxed a little and stayed with Pierre to support him; although he also didn't know what to expect. He'd remembered his first and only interview with Madame Moreau when he'd asked if he could volunteer his skills at the school. Frightened at the time, he was most grateful of the opportunity. It had given him a worthwhile career. Gaston opened the conversation.

"Hello Pierre. I'm so pleased to be able to meet with you today and to give you information about my restaurant."

Pierre's nerves had stolen his voice and he had difficulty replying. He nodded instead.

Gaston proceeded to inform them how he'd been apprenticed to a much-celebrated chef in an elegant restaurant in Paris. He spoke of how he'd worked hard and long hours doing what he loved best. Gastronomy governed his life then and it still did now. It was his passion; so much so that he'd written numerous books on the theoretical and practical approach to food and culture. Included in his books were recipes which he'd perfected when acquiring his expertise with different chefs during his rigorous training. He was proud of the fact that some large hotel chains in Paris and other regions in France, used his delectable recipes.

Both Pierre and Hugo were fascinated with Gaston's reminiscing of his illustrious career.

"So, Pierre. Do you think you would like to work with us here?"

Pierre nodded again; willing his disinclined voice-box to generate an adequate answer.

"Yes", he uttered.

Hugo looked over at Pierre, pressing him to provide more information about himself.

Taking a deep breath, Pierre quickly recited the words he'd been rehearsing for days.

"Yes. I would like, very much, to work with you. Firstly though, I would like to inform you that I am autistic and if I don't make eye contact or look away from you when you are speaking to me, it's because I find it difficult. It's not my intention to be discourteous to you. I am thankful to you for taking the time to speak with me."

Hugo sighed. Pierre had done it!

"Thank you, Pierre, for informing me about how you present yourself. It's helpful for me. I'm led to believe that you're interested in cooking and you have ambitions to become a chef."

"Yes, Monsieur Lemaire. My mother taught me how to cook and bake. She taught me many of her traditional recipes, which I've adapted into my own style. I like my food to be artistically arranged on the plate. I have been influenced by Bocus and

Millau."

Gaston grinned. His unexpected, extended answer had surprised him; and Hugo! Gaston had also been heavily influenced by their Nouvelle Cuisine techniques.

"I've brought some photographs to show you. It's my own modern perspective on how I think healthy food should be cooked and served. The photographs were taken each time I produced something new and every time I served my cuisine at family dinners. Would you like to take a look?"

Without waiting for a reply, he excitedly passed his portfolio to Gaston.

"Most certainly, Pierre. Thank you."

Gaston turned the pages, stopping now and again to concentrate on a specific presentation. He was impressed with the manner in which Pierre had made notes at the side of each photograph. He'd also used the same format to record his own recipes.

They watched in anticipation as the chef nodded his head and smiled.

Admiring the young man's inventive flair, Gaston could visualise a younger version of himself in Pierre. He could see great potential and he'd already made his decision. If Pierre would be a willing and committed apprentice, then he'd take him under his wing as his protégé. He'd instil in him all the qualities and obligatory skills that would be required, if he was to become as equally, if not more, successful as himself.

"I'm impressed with your work, Pierre. It's not my usual practice to do this, but I'd like you to come to work with me here. Firstly, you will work in the kitchen, learning all aspects relating to food preparation and hygiene regulations. Those tasks will give you the grounding and help you to clearly understand what is required of you, if you are to become a chef. It's hard work, you know. If I can see that you are totally committed, I'll offer you an apprenticeship. I do understand that you have to complete your schooling, but if you are willing to work some evenings and at the weekend, you will gain much experience."

Open-mouthed and eyes wide open, Pierre and Hugo hadn't anticipated Gaston's immediate offer. Pierre's hands were shaking and he tried, unsuccessfully, to refrain from tapping his fingers on the side of the chair.

"I'm willing to do that, Monsieur Lemaire. I can start work immediately. I have already taken my exams. I am waiting for my results"

After pressing his hands tightly together and shaking them, for a few moments, he extended his right hand to Gaston and shook his hand.

"Thank you Monsieur Lemaire. Thank you for giving me this excellent opportunity."

Gaston was euphoric with the thought of having the opportunity to develop yet another protégé. From viewing Pierre's work, he could see that he already had an extraordinary talent; one which could be cultivated even further. He would personally facilitate his evolvement into becoming a celebrated chef. Yes, Gaston was extremely excited and more than eager to teach this young man everything he knew!

Rising from his seat, he turned towards his new protégé and smiled.

"My manager will contact you tomorrow in the afternoon with more details. I look forward to you joining my restaurant. Thank you for coming."

Pierre nodded his head and bowed.

"Thank you again, Monsieur Lemaire."

Stunned by their recent experience, Pierre and Hugo watched Gaston as he returned to the kitchen. Both remained silent, taking in what had just happened. The unanticipated, immediate offer of employment had seemed unreal.

Pierre's hyperfocusing on his cooking had paid off! His repetitive, unwavering enthusiasm had produced perfection. Inwardly, he felt proud. It was at that precise moment, that he thought of all the people who'd criticised him for his relentless obsession with perfection; and he suddenly felt convinced that he could become a chef!

CHAPTER TWELVE
October

When Pierre returned to school that afternoon, he immediately briefed the others on the interview and how well it had gone.

The students listened attentively as he described, in great detail, the interview process and what had occurred afterwards.

His feedback was welcomed, as the other students would be interviewed later in the week. Much encouraged by Pierre's successful outcome, the room was buzzing with anticipation.

Serge had been instrumental in getting his friends to co-operate and become involved in the project. They'd all been briefed on the purpose for the placing of the students in an understanding and welcoming environment.

As Pierre was answering several questions from his excited peers, the door opened slowly and Madame Moreau entered.

"Well, Pierre. How was your interview?"

Pierre's broad smile gave her the answer she was anticipating. Hurriedly, he relayed all of the information he'd given to the others earlier.

Hugo nodded in acknowledgement, as he confirmed Pierre's account of the event.

"Congratulations. I'm very pleased for you."

Such instant success was encouraging. It was vital information for her progress file; which she'd proudly present to the school inspector on his next visit.

Hugo gave permission for the students to leave early.

When they'd left, she again approached the subject of him working extra hours.

"The work you are doing with the students is outstanding. Would you consider doing an extra day's teaching?"

"Thank you for your compliment, but I want to devote some time to my family and I have a project of my own which needs attending to. I'll do some work from home, for the new intake."

She'd known what the answer would be; but she had to ask, just in case! She was thankful for his offer work from home. It was important that the project be kept on target.

****

By late Friday afternoon, all those who had been interviewed, had gained placements.

One girl was going to work in a local bakery and another had gained a position in the adjoining café/patisserie.

The young man, who'd initially been scared of being interviewed, was going to work on a farm.

Cecile, now much more confident, had been offered a position in the local Mairie's office.

Another student had gained a placement working in a *cave*, learning the fundamentals of winemaking.

The seventh student had been given a probationary contract of employment with a large computer software organisation in Narbonne.

Overjoyed with the outcome, Hugo was aware that he couldn't have accomplished any of the placements, without the help of Suzette and Serge.

CHAPTER THIRTEEN
November

Sarah welcomed those valued times when Hugo wasn't in work; especially the occasions when Nico wasn't in school. Although she knew that it was essential that he developed a curriculum for the new school intake, she sometimes felt a little resentful at the amount of time he expended on it.

He'd also spent endless hours sifting through candidate applications for the teaching positions. It was imperative that those chosen for interview, had the right blend of experience, understanding of difference and an innovative approach to the way they taught.

It had been his intention that the new recruits would commence three weeks before the new intake of pupils, so that they could become familiar with the curriculum and the environment, but he knew that may not be possible, as they'd have to give notice of their intention to leave from their place of work.

Pupil intake, collaboration with parents and the school inspectorate was time-consuming, but it had been worth the effort. It had been agreed that only twelve children would be allowed into the unit at one given time.

Depending on the severity of learning difference and disability, Hugo had advised, with Suzette's assistance, on the ratio of pupil to each teacher; to ensure that each pupil received the appropriate attention.

Whilst he acknowledged that the setting up of the unit was important, he was also aware of the effect on his own well-being. He was looking forward to the time when the unit was up and running. Then he could spend some welcome time with his family.

He was aware that Nico, whilst quite able to entertain himself, could be demanding at times when things didn't go to plan. His tantrums could be unmanageable and it seemed, to Sarah, that only when he was with his father, that his moods were calmer.

She felt somewhat inadequate on those occasions. The differences in mother and son's understanding of behaviour and attitudes seemed to clash. She'd thought she was becoming more aware of his idiosyncrasies and more adept at dealing with his rigid habits.

In times of contemplation, she'd remind herself that her brain worked in a different way to her son's.

If she was honest with herself, not only did she feel inadequate at times, she also felt like an outsider in her own family. When Hugo and Nico were having some time together, they understood each other perfectly and they'd sit for several hours, discussing topics which were of interest to them; writing poetry and singing, whilst tinkling the ivories.

Jealousy wasn't part of her nature or even a word which she would consider using; but she did wish that she could grasp the workings of their minds and join in with some of their intellectual conversations.

Nevertheless, more than appreciative that her husband and son shared an inseparable bond, her love for them over-rode her own feelings of unawareness and, sometimes rejection.

Over the last six years, she'd experienced how an autist may feel in a neurotypical's world and it was confusing and uncomfortable at times.

On occasions when Nico had been shopping with her, he'd sometimes strike up inappropriate conversations with people in the supermarket. People, unaccepting of his difference, would think him an oddity and precocious with his formal tone of voice. As young as he was, her son knew he was different and could sense what they were thinking.

Once, on the way home in the car, he'd asked her why people thought there was something wrong with him.

Recalling the conversation, she shuddered.

"Maman. Is there something wrong with me? You and Père said that my autism was part of who I am."

"No, darling. There's nothing wrong with you. Yes, it is. You're unique."

"Then why do people stare at me and pull faces when I speak to them? They should not do that, should they? I was only asking them if they knew why volcanoes erupt. I was going to tell them that they erupt to release pressure that builds up inside the earth and explain how they could tell the difference between magma and lava. They walked away from me. I know that they think I am weird."

She'd seen what had happened. She could fully understand why they did what they did. They'd probably wondered why this child was spouting on about volcanoes and rock formation in a very formal, upper-class English voice.

She'd heard one woman say, "Let's go. There's something not quite right with him. It's a shame. He's a bit retarded. Where's his mother?"

She'd also seen the confused look on her child's face. Nico's current fascination was with volcanoes and he'd stay in his bedroom for long periods, researching everything he could find about them. In a few months, his new fixation could be a desire to research space travel, ocean creatures or climate history.

"No, they shouldn't, darling. They may not understand that everyone is different, in one way or another."

"I cannot see why they do not understand, Maman? I do not like it. It offends me. It hurts me to think I am doing something wrong."

She inhaled deeply and then exhaled before speaking.

"Nico. It's just how some people are. Don't worry about it."

He wouldn't give up.

"Maman, I disagree. Not all people are like that. You cannot give me a straight answer. At times, I do not understand the way you think."

Being a neurotypical mother was draining, especially when relating to her child's direct questioning and his 'need-to-know now' approach. Even more so, when she found it difficult to explain what she wanted to say.

Since that event, she'd thought long and hard about what he'd said. Her own child was educating her on the complexities of autism. He was right. People *didn't* understand. Being autistic didn't mean that her son didn't feel affronted by their reactions. He did! She was glad he was able to confidently voice his opinion, instead of keeping it to himself.

She'd found that many neurotypicals could be delusional in their judgement of autism. If they just stopped for a moment to analyse their own behaviours, like she had, then they may find out that they also possess similar autistic traits.

She wished that people would recognise that their idle comments and judgements were unjustifiably harmful and disrespectful.

She walked outside, towards where they were both chatting inside the summer house. Deciding against approaching them, she hovered in the background and listened to her son questioning his père.

A warm breeze welcomed her, bringing with it the scent of Hugo's cologne. She inhaled deeply and smiled.

Considering it was November, there would still been plenty of sunny days; still warm enough to be outdoors enjoying the fresh air.

This specific area in the garden was a peaceful place; one which looked out onto fields and the mountains in the distance. It adequately fed the imagination and was good for relaxing.

Nico had been re-writing his poem and was momentarily asking his père to approve it. Gaining others' approval was a part of his self-doubt. Her son needed endless amounts of reassurance for his efforts; especially following his piano recitals.

At certain times, his juxtaposed confidence and neediness was confusing for her.

"Do you know that Carcassonne Castle has fifty two towers and the walls around it are three kilometres long?"

"I do, son. How do you know that?"

"Grand-père told me when I was writing my poem with him. He also told me that a man named Gustave Nadaud wrote a poem about Carcassonne. We are going to do some research about him and his poetry next time I go over to see him."

Her child's capacity to retain information that he was interested in, didn't compare with his inability to remember what he classed as being 'unimportant' details. She speculated on whether Carcassonne Castle would be his next intense focus of interest.

"Would you two like a drink and something to eat?"

Startled by her presence, he stared directly into her eyes and waited a while before answering.

Sarah, anticipating his predictable answer, waited patiently for his reply; the one he used frequently when he was interrupted.

"Maman. May I remind you that it is not very polite to interrupt when people are speaking. We are very busy discussing my poem."

Raising her eyebrows, she feigned surprise.

"Is there something wrong with your eyes?"

Once more, he hadn't correctly interpreted her body language.

Hugo, also aware of Nico's familiar retorts, spoke firmly to his son. Even though he knew that his literal way of processing neurotypical behaviour was part of who his son was, he still wasn't happy with the manner in which he sometimes spoke to Sarah.

She didn't take his abruptness personally. She realised that her unannounced appearance had alarmed him.

Many times, throughout his own childhood, Hugo had felt alienated, awkward and vulnerable; not being able to explain himself and understand why things made him feel confused, uncomfortable and frightened.

"Nico, it's rude to speak to your maman in that way. She was only asking if we'd like to eat some lunch."

"Père, when I interrupt others, you inform me that it is not socially correct. I am only doing what you and Grand-mère have taught me to do."

Sarah felt sad for her son; his literalness and his assumption that everyone thought like he did would, in no doubt, get him into trouble as he got older and started to mix more in neurotypical, social environments.

The mingled messages he was receiving, confused him even more. He was being given the impression that it was acceptable for someone to interrupt him, but it was most definitely *not* appropriate for him to interrupt anyone else!

Later, when he was a little older, Hugo would share more of his own experiences with his son, so that he too wouldn't feel misunderstood or ignored. He didn't want him to mask his fears, like he'd done. He wanted him to talk openly about them.

Hugo made the decision.

"Yes, ma chérie. We are ready to eat now. Writing poetry is hungry work!"

Nico's recurring, amplified fear of upsetting people had sent him begging for forgiveness. He ran towards Sarah and clung onto her. Apologising profusely, he needed more reassurance.

"I am sorry. I did not mean to be impolite. I am sorry for being naughty."

Her heart melted. She lifted him up into her arms and kissed him.

"I know you didn't, Nico. You don't have to keep saying sorry. Once is enough."

"I love you, Maman. Do you know that?"

As he snuggled in closer and clung onto her neck, a tear escaped and trickled down to the side of her mouth and she wiped it away.

"Yes, I do know."

Once he'd been comforted, he struggled to be released from her hold and hurried back to Hugo.

Sarah looked towards her husband and he nodded.

"Shall I give it to her now, Père?"

"Yes, if you want to."

She looked puzzled.

"Close your eyes, Maman and hold out your hands. I have something for you."

He stood in front of her and placed the small statuette in her hands; a replica of the one which Hugo had sculpted of himself and his own maman after she'd died.

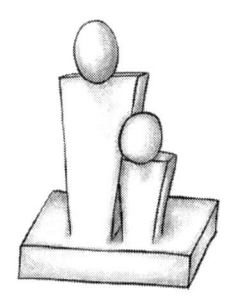

As she opened her eyes, she was amazed to see what he'd given her.

"I wanted you to have one like the one in the garden, but I am not old enough to make one so large, so Grand-père helped me to make this one. I carved most of it myself, though. Do you like it, Maman?"

"Like it. I love it, Nico."

Although she was well aware, that her child wasn't singularly talented, she was pleased to see that he also had an aptitude for sculpting.

He allowed her another quick cuddle before he struggled to be released again.

"I'll bring lunch out here and we can eat on the terrace. Are you warm enough, or shall we eat inside?"

"We're ok to eat out here, ma chérie."

Grasping the miniature sculpture, she held it close to her chest. She'd treasure it for the rest of her life!

As she entered the kitchen, she knew her son was as confused as she was at times. Getting used to his habits was demanding, but at least her child was in touch with his emotions. She'd learnt, from reading endless amounts of textbooks and from speaking to other mothers, that some autists had difficulty with being tactile and even articulating their emotions.

Sarah had also learned, over time, to adjust her own expectations of her husband and her son; constantly remaining conscious of acknowledging their competent peculiarities, instead of focusing on their dissimilarities.

Whatever their differences, she knew that she respected both of them. The merging of their neurodiverse and neurotypical worlds, with the help of Suzette, Serge and a few close friends, functioned quite successfully in most instances.

Yet, there was still much to learn!

CHAPTER FOURTEEN
December

Serge had spoken with his friend Guy, who was the mayor in Lezignan, to enquire whether Nico could be involved in the annual Christmas Concert, with the possibility of raising some funds for the people in India.

The schedule for the event had already been completed. However, Guy had suggested that he performed in the interval.

With Serge's help, Nico had been practicing Christmas classical concertos and was excited to perform.

The concert took place mid-afternoon on Christmas Eve. It had been raining all the previous week and there had been a strong easterly wind, which made it feel colder than it was. All tickets had been sold and the hall was packed with adults and children, all eager to participate in the Christmas celebrations.

Following readings, recitals and singing of Christmas carols, Guy announced that there would be an interval. He also introduced Nico.

The little boy stood in front of the large piano and addressed the audience, first in French and then in English.

"I am going to be playing some Christmas music for you this evening. I do hope that you will like it. If you do like it, may I ask if you would kindly make a donation to the people in India, who do not have clean water to drink. The children are dying because they have diseases. My Grandmére's friends went to India this year to help them and they told me all about it."

Guy lifted him onto the platform and then set him down on the stool, wondering if his legs would reach the pedals. As he adjusted his posture and stretched out his legs, Nico's small frame seemed lost behind the large piano.

His first piece was from Mozart's Sleigh Ride. As his small fingers skillfully caressed the keys, it was as if a sleigh was gliding over the snow.

Without interruption, he went straight into Corelli's Christmas Concerto, delivering his music with so much emotional directness. There was a palpable, calming atmosphere within the hall, as he creatively illustrated the biblical story of the birth of Jesus through his wonderful rendition.

Finally, he glided effortlessly into Handel's Messiah. Eyebrows were raised and short intakes of breath could be heard as Nico moved in and out of sections of the oratorio.

He waved one of his hands from side to side, encouraging the audience to join in and sing the Hallelujah Chorus.

People got up from their seats and started singing loudly. They remained standing until Nico had finished and Guy had helped his down from his stool.

Bowing graciously several times, in front of the applauding audience, he acknowledged the positive reception.

"Merci. Joyeux Noel. Thank you very much. Happy Christmas to you all."

Resounding 'bravos' and loud hand-clapping continued to echo through the hall.

Hugo, who was stood at the rear of the hall, heard someone comment, "However could a small child like him, play such powerful music? He's a genius."

Aware of coins and notes being tossed into collecting baskets and being passed along the rows of seats, he was delighted that his son had fulfilled his promise!

CHAPTER FIFTEEN
January 2018

Replies to the job adverts had been received. After careful sifting of the applicants' suitability for the positions, several interviews had been undertaken, positions had been offered and acceptances had been received. The teachers had to provide their employers with three months' notice and so they'd only be able to commence teaching after Easter.

They'd agreed to come over to Lezignan in the February half-term to participate in some training. Whilst considering the uniformity of French educational law, Hugo had carefully designed a curriculum to suit each pupil's differing needs.

He hadn't embarked on anything like this before. With the help of Suzette, who had a vast experience of working with learning differences before she'd retired and his own sizeable amount of research into different-needs teaching methods, he'd succeeding in formulating a plan which he was certain would work.

Two of the newly-recruited teachers were female and of English descent, with a wide-ranging experience of working within specialist schools in England. They also spoke French.

The other teacher was male and of French descent. Having taught in Paris at a school for autistic children, he'd returned home to Lezignan to help his family care for his younger brother, who was autistic.

The choice of teachers was intentional. All had displayed an innate confidence in their creative ability to differentiate their teaching methods.

It was thought that the English teachers' unconventional understanding and knowledge of difference, would blend well with the planned holistic techniques and enrichment activities.

The native-French teacher would, in turn, bring his own extensive knowledge of meaningful education for autistic children.

To eliminate any unnecessary stress for the children, informal school-entry interviews were held. Accompanied by their parents, each child was gently encouraged to join in a brief discussion, initially to establish clear communication links, but essentially to identify existing strengths, insights and differing needs.

Hugo had gained permission for Nico to be

considered for entry into the school. Whilst he didn't want anyone to assume that preferential treatment was being given, his son also had his own needs and he'd undergo the entry procedure like the other children.

Throughout his interview, Nico expressed his misperception of the questions which were asked.

"Père, pardon. I mean Monsieur Couture, why are you asking me these questions, when you know all about me?"

Amused at his direct questioning, the other teachers tried to conceal their laughter.

"Nico, it's a requirement that all pupils go through the initial interview, so that the teachers will be aware of everyone's needs. It is important."

He stared at them; an element of surprise exposed within his deep-brown eyes.

Acknowledging an exact mirroring of his own mannerisms in those of his only child, Hugo felt a sudden surge of fatherly tenderness towards him.

After the interviews had taken place, it was decided that there would be an intake of children with differing levels of abilities and disabilities, in line with the school's inclusive ethos.

Under no illusions, the teachers had a clear vision of the challenges ahead of them.

His son had been accepted into the school. There would now be no need for him to be tutored at home. Moreover, Enzo had also been accepted.

CHAPTER SIXTEEN
May

Training sessions had been undertaken. Teachers and parents worked closely to discuss and plan how individualised support would be implemented.

The purpose of including the parents was to reduce any angst and to illustrate the benefits that their children would gain. By attending the school, they'd be taught in a progressive, safe environment where they'd be offered varied experiences.

Some of the sessions had been delivered by a welfare, speech and behavioural therapist, who'd been recruited because of the huge success she'd achieved in schools in England. Luckily, Nancy Leo was fluent in French and was also qualified to administer medication if necessary.

One particularly interesting session on how to

closely monitor and manage disruptive behaviour – due to a difference in routine – was helpful for all of them. Parents had welcomed the technique, as they'd regularly experienced problems when trying to manage their children's meltdowns.

Within the sessions, all were reminded of how instructions needed to be precise; especially so, for those children who were literal and misinterpreted information.

Suzette's background in inclusive education, had been instrumental in her designing a flexible curricula with Hugo and the other teachers.

A less rigid, individualised approach was to be adopted; coupled with a more structured focus on the children understanding school rules, routines and expectations.

All lessons and tasks had been designed with the children's fears and concerns about school in mind. As well as helping them to cope with change, creative lessons would be included on a daily basis, to alleviate boredom for those who were visual learners and higher functioning.

Following careful consideration and several, lengthy discussions with parents, it was agreed that an Applied Behavioural Therapy approach would be implemented.

With endorsement from Nancy, Suzette had stressed that it wouldn't be a one-size fits all method of teaching. It would be adapted for each child.

Gilbert, who was streets ahead of other

medical professionals in the early diagnosis of autism, was also supportive of using behavioural therapies as a means of empowering the children.

Primarily, a goal would be identified. Then the child would work towards that goal. When the learning outcome had been achieved, a meaningful reward would be given.

The model was not too dissimilar to those used within mainstream schools, where star and smiley faces stickers, watching movies and extra playtimes were used as effective motivators.

This proven method had revealed that children had achieved specific outcomes more quickly, rather than when they were hyperfocusing on repetitive activities.

Initially, the discussions had provoked mixed concerns. Not surprisingly, some parents thought that the school may be trying to normalise their children by suppressing their children's behaviours. They didn't want them to feel even more anxious and uncomfortable.

In turn, there was a risk that the extra anxiety would further increase the parents' stress levels. Social ignorance had already resulted in several mothers in the locality, having to take prescribed medication to help with their mental health.

Other parents thought that it would help their children to function more effectively and the approach would not necessarily change who they were. They knew that they were lucky that their children had been given a place in the school; there was a lengthy waiting list! In fact, they were all relieved to hear that co-teaching would take place.

In an attempt to develop the children's self-confidence and boost their communication skills, a proportionate amount of learning would take place in the playground. It was accepted that some may find social interaction demanding, but its purpose was to create a sense of belonging.

As a result of the intensive training, a parents' support group had been formed. Several parents wanted to become advocates for their children and they'd agreed to introduce them to more social activities outside of school.

Within the group discussions, they openly and honestly spoke of how they'd been faced with ridicule and social isolation within the communities where they lived. Their quality of life had been affected.

Visiting public places had been problematic for them; especially when they'd had to cope with their children having unexpected meltdowns, due to their immediate reactions to sensory overload. On those occasions, the harassed parents had endured severe criticism for not disciplining their children enough.

Their mental health had suffered and family relationships had broken down due to the stress of raising an autistic child; resulting in exhausted single mothers and fathers being left to muddle through the daily issues; all of which had occurred through a lack of acceptance and misunderstanding of others.

A few parents admitted that they didn't want people to know that their children were autistic and they'd gone to great lengths to hide the fact that they were, so that they wouldn't be judged.

Previous attempts to persuade their children to change their behaviours, had produced hardly any change and the unhappy children continued having their uncontrollable meltdowns.

Yet, in spite of their many challenges, the group were determined to alter societal attitudes towards their children's differences. To encourage the villagers to be more inclusive, they'd already arranged some small events to raise awareness and funds for the school.

With parental involvement, there was now hope that there'd be a significant transformation in the children's education and well-being.

CHAPTER SEVENTEEN
May

The new intake of pupils assembled in the school hall with their parents.

Some were skipping and others were jumping up and down. Others just clung onto their parents, expressionless.

Although the building was large, it was divided in such a way that it would make the transition from primary (école) to secondary (collège unique and lycée) education much easier: rather than the children having to move into another unfamiliar building.

Hugo and Madame Moreau stood in front of the group. Although he would be heavily involved in rolling out and monitoring the project, Hugo was still responsible for teaching the older children.

The teachers, together with Suzette and Nancy, stood behind them, listening and watching. When the important information about school hours, break times and alone-times had been relayed, they introduced themselves and spoke about what they would be teaching.

One boy had heard enough. He wasn't happy being in close proximity to others and he decided to get up from his chair and shuffle along the walls around the room.

His mother tried, unsuccessfully, to bring him back to his chair. His agitation increased and he pushed her.

Hugo nodded towards her, indicating that it was ok for him to remain there. She sat down.

Nico was watching and wanted to go over to him, but his père shook his head and so he stayed where he was.

Another boy started scratching himself and began rocking backwards and forwards. He, also, was feeling threatened and wanted to go home.

"Maman, je veux aller a la maison", he begged.

Her inability to soothe him in these unfamiliar surroundings was distressing to witness.

At the front of the group, a girl began to hum. She was hearing impaired and frightened by the different location and repeatedly pressed the heart-shaped drawing on the back of her hand. Her mother also had one on her hand. The heart signified her mother's love for her and she felt better when she pressed it.

The atmosphere within the hall was becoming strained. It was only to be expected.

As the teachers moved forward to try to calm the children, one boy broke free from his mother's restraint and started to run speedily around the room. She waited for her son to go past her and caught him by his arm.

Expecting a meltdown, she tried to soothe him as he started kicking and hitting her.

Aware that the child's behaviour was because he was out of his comfort zone, Hugo went over to assist her.

Planted deep within his psyche were the negative educational experiences of his childhood. It had been tough, but he'd survived it. If it had been easy, his life may have taken a different path. He may not have had the time to spend with his mother before she died.

"He's been removed from his other schools, mainly because of his disruptive behaviour", she explained.

He could resonate with the word 'disruptive'.

"It's ok. Let's get him outside."

Whilst all this was happening, the rest of the teaching staff had moved towards the group and had encouraged some of them to go into the playground.

Nico approached the boy who'd been shuffling against the walls. He wanted to befriend him and gently touched his arm. His teacher had asked him to 'buddy' him.

The boy quivered and began clapping his hands frantically.

In his usual formal tone, Nico asked the boy his name.

"Pardon. Je suis Nico. Que lest votre nom?"

The boy edged away and glared menacingly.

He asked again; this time in a softer tone.

"Que lest votre nom?"

Reluctantly, he muttered, "Xavier."

In time, he had a strong feeling that he and Xavier would become friends. His grand-mère had taught him about values and being kind to others and he'd put into practice what he'd learnt.

Outside, Enzo had also been trying to 'buddy up' with the boy who'd been running around the hall in an effort to dispel his nervous energy. The boy was now running around the playground at an Olympic speed and Enzo had trouble keeping up with him.

The other pupils and parents were shown around the classrooms and then taken into the quiet zones where soft, background music was playing.

For the teaching staff, although somewhat expected, the commotion relating to the children's fears, had been a baptism of fire

Aware that routine was imperative and would need to be established as soon as was practically possible, they were determined to do everything they could to make it happen.

CHAPTER EIGHTEEN
May

His formal tone and his flipping in and out of two languages confused them.

The children wondered why he spoke that way. His directness and mature style of speaking was off-putting for them and, also for the teachers at times; even though they'd previously been made fully aware of his differences.

Lessons for him and Enzo, had to be made more challenging to prevent them from becoming demotivated. They were given responsibilities and both deemed their classroom duties a privilege.

Nico's duty was to ensure that the children wrote their names on the board when they came into class; assisting them if they were anxious.

Enzo had been given the duty of handing out

flash cards with symbols on, to help with improving communication skills.

Being a rigid routiner, Nico seemed to be unaware of the small changes he was making to accommodate his new friend. Conversation with him was a problem at times, as his friend had difficulty with pronunciation and couldn't get his words out; but Nico was patient and listened.

He'd wait for him inside the school gate on a morning and walk into school with him. He'd sit with him at lunchtimes and try to help him with academic tasks. Xavier would continually drop his pencil and hide under his desk, with the pretence of not being able to find it. He found it hard to retain any simple facts that weren't of interest to him.

Uncannily, he could identify the tiniest of images on the pages of his reading book, but had difficulty reading and sounding out the words. He didn't like making mistakes in his writing and he'd cross out his work if it was incorrect, starting over and over again until there were no mistakes on the paper.

His repetitive, rushed practice of working was time consuming. There wasn't an occasion when his work would be free of scribbles and crossing out. Almost always, he'd rip up his worksheet and run off, complaining of a headache.

It was at those times that Nico would follow him and attempt to calm him down.

"You can do this. Grand-mère says that a

person cannot be good at everything, but if we do our best, then that is all we can do."

He'd even managed to get Xavier interested in music; encouraging him to sit beside him and sing along as he played the piano. Nico had also urged his friend to draw some images of how he was feeling and had persuaded him to point to them, when he didn't want to talk.

Sometimes, they'd just sit quietly together, without speaking.

It had taken quite a while for the children to integrate into their new surroundings. Initially, the classroom was an extremely noisy, disruptive place. Some children refused to join in lessons, because of the noise. One girl could hear the fluorescent light making a whining sound and it annoyed her. They were taken along to social withdrawal areas for alone-time.

Another boy had a defiant behaviour and he'd become irritable when asked to do something he didn't want to do. He'd get up from his chair and storm off, shouting No, No, No.

At the end of those early school days, both the children and the teachers were exhausted. All were learning to adapt, trying to cope with the changes.

On chaotic days, when several meltdowns occurred, some children were ushered into the hall for music lessons. Those who were hypersensitive to noise, were taken to the quiet area and given headphones to wear, to block out the noise.

At times, it would almost seem that Nico was in charge of the lesson, as he played the piano and ordered the children to sing along; correcting them if they missed words out or sang the wrong tune.

Depending on the type of music he played, his enchanting, natural ability to manipulate the piano keys would either calm them or stimulate them.

Whatever their behaviour, they were temporarily distracted from their sensory issues. The teacher was grateful for Nico's contribution.

It was overwhelming to watch the children with their eclectic mix of complex personalities, all sitting quietly or stomping their feet to the rhythm. When upbeat music was played, one wheelchair user would spin himself around. Another child, who was without speech, would hum along and tap her feet; sometimes even managing to utter the odd word.

After a few months, the applied behaviour techniques had led to continual improvements in some of the children. Their language skills had improved and the children became accustomed to the new methods of learning, new routines and their new friends.

Goals were achieved within the timescales, mainly because they were small and achievable - and involved rewards. Boundaries were challenged and children were encouraged to take some risks; much to the wrath of some overprotective parents.

With the assistance of Suzette, Hugo had introduced mindfulness into the school curriculum.

At the end of the afternoon lessons, all the children sat for fifteen minutes. Several of the younger children fidgeted and couldn't sit still. It didn't matter. The process of just sitting there was what mattered. It was some down-time in their lives before they went home.

CHAPTER NINETEEN
June

Even though he'd become more sociable at school, Nico still needed to have his own space to switch off, read his books and work on new music. His inspiration for his new compositions was taken from the spectacular view just outside his bedroom window.

Whilst reading in his room, he'd heard them arguing and had crept to the top of the stairs to listen. He'd never heard them quarrel before.

"I was only saying that I think you've been working too much lately and then when you come home, you go off over to the labyrinth in Serge's clearing or into the garden on your own."

"So, what's the problem?"

"The problem is that we don't seem to have

time together these days. I want to spend some time with you, like we used to."

Raising his eyebrows, he sighed heavily.

"What do you mean? We do spend some time together. We spend time together when I'm not in work, don't we?"

As a neurotypical spouse, she assumed that she was being clear about her needs; obviously not clear enough!

Not reading her signals, he was annoyed with what she'd said, especially when he'd had a very stressful day at work.

"You know what I mean."

"No. I don't know what you mean, Sarah. Stop playing mind games. Just tell me straight. What's on your mind? You know how I function. Remember? We're not from the same planet."

"I just feel as if you've been neglecting our relationship; neglecting me."

Inasmuch as she felt unheard, he equally felt unheard. He was confused. She hadn't given him any previous indication of there being a problem.

Not wanting more confrontation, he turned his back on her, momentarily incapable of admitting anything.

"Well, say something Hugo."

"I don't have anything to say to you."

He opened the door and stormed out.

Sighing, she watched him go. Sometimes, she wondered if it was all worth it. Sometimes she wished he wasn't autistic and she didn't have to try so hard; to know when not to disturb his train of thought. In spite of their good intentions, the fractious miscommunications between them both were wounding for her and perplexing for him. Sometimes, she wished she didn't love him so much; but she did, with a passion!

Setting aside some time with each other was part of their usual routine. Nico would stay over at his grandparents and they would re-connect; going over their individual lists of things that needed to be discussed, listening to each other, drinking wine and making love. But due to his work, they hadn't been able to find time for each other.

Lists and notes were as much a part of Hugo's life as they were of Nico's; they were displayed all around the house. The important colour coding system, which they'd devised when they first met, had lapsed somewhat. Notes that were urgent were highlighted in red. Not-so-urgent notes were highlighted in green and the notes which were highlighted in yellow, didn't have a timescale.

It suddenly dawned on her that she should've been marking the notes with a red highlighter pen. She'd meant to buy a new one a few weeks ago and had forgotten. That was the reason for his misunderstanding. She felt totally responsible.

Meandering along the lane, he pondered on Sarah's style of processing and compared her way of thinking to his own. Could 'reading between the lines' be considered a strength? Could his own neurodiverse thoughts be considered inappropriate and a weakness? No. He deduced that there was no right answer. They were just two different ways of processing and, misinterpreting the information. They both saw things from their own critical viewpoints.

Whilst Sarah was in the kitchen making his birthday cake, Nico stealthily crept down the stairs, tiptoeing silently through the sprawling living room and out through the open door. Running along the lane, he caught up with Hugo.

"Wait. I am coming with you."

"Did you hear us arguing?"

"Yes. Why did you walk out? Are you going to leave us?"

Looking down at his own mirror image, he saw the confusion and fear etched on his son's face as he knelt down to face him.

"No. I'm not going to leave you. We were just discussing my work. It'll be ok."

Nico grabbed his père's hand and held it tight. He didn't want him to go. Neither did he want his maman to be sad.

Distracting his son from the upset, he picked him up and held him close, before putting him down again.

"Come. Let's walk."

Father and son strolled, hand in hand down the quiet, country lanes surrounding their house. Together, they discussed environment issues and current world affairs; enlightening each other with snippets of facts that they'd recently learnt.

Holding his père's hand was reassuring for Nico. Hugo couldn't ever remember holding onto his birth father's hand. He'd held Serge's hand on several occasions. The strength of his grip had been reassuring in times of desperation. They had their own unique system of understanding. At times, if they didn't want to speak, they'd use gestures or hand signs to indicate or confirm. A firm squeeze of the hand was all it would take to confirm their inseparable bond.

They trusted and believed in each other. Hugo genuinely believed that his son could make a difference to others' lives. He already was!

"Père, I have been reading another article on climate change and how it is affecting our world. It stated that people are destroying the planet. We have to do something about it now."

He wasn't surprised by his statement. It was usual for his son to want to discuss something about what was happening in the world. For a child of his age, he had an exceptional knowledge of world events.

Suzette had recently taken Nico along to an educational centre to complete a computer-based IQ test. His results had been astounding. After answering numerous multiple-choice questions for an hour, a printed report showed that his IQ level had been recorded at 169. They were delighted with the results, although not surprised with the score. His savant gifts were already proof enough!

"Yes, I agree. We do have to make changes.

The greenhouse gases are having drastic effects on the earth. That's why there are floods in Asia and the ice is melting in the Arctic region. We need to try and reduce the greenhouse effect."

"We do need some greenhouse gases for the earth, though. The trees and plants need it for photosynthesis. The gases keep the planet warm. Otherwise, the earth would be too cold."

They continued to discuss the effects of global warming as they strayed from the country lanes and onto the canal bank; with Nico adopting the adult role of questioning and providing a more detailed answer than was necessary.

Hugo had encouraged his son's connection with nature, ever since he was a toddler. He loved growing vegetables in his own little patch and was now cultivating his very own compost heap. He'd sit for long periods in the garden, listening to the sounds of the birds and deciding which new plants he'd like to grow.

Visiting the seaside and walking through the forested areas around the Canal du Midi, were other pastimes that he loved.

"Does your maman know that you followed me?"

"No. I sneaked out. I was very quiet."

Hugo was concerned. If Sarah had noticed that Nico was missing, she'd be anxious.

"I think we'd better go back home now. Your maman will be wondering where we are. Come, I'll race you back. See if you can win me, again!"

Unaware of Suzette's presence on the other side of the hedge, they laughed as they ran.

She'd watched them strolling hand in hand, many times, whilst pottering in her garden.

As on other occasions, she'd witnessed the true nature of their auras. Her auric sight had been developed over the years and she could easily tune into auras around people, plants and other items.

Bright green in colour, Nico's aura was so significant, being that he was a creative individual. His strong connection with nature and his concern about preservation of the planet was indicative of his heartfelt desire to help and heal everything. When his aura was a dull green, she knew that he was at odds with the world; and those times could be quite frequent.

Hugo's aura was usually a bright yellow, tinged with green. Dotingly, she recalled how he had become more intuitive, especially since the death of his maman.

Unsurprisingly, Serge's aura was the same colour; both being creative and intelligent beings.

Happier, now that Hugo's mood was much lighter than when she'd first seen Nico join him on the lane, she continued gathering wild strawberries that were nestling amongst the hedgerows.

CHAPTER TWENTY
July

It had been another exhausting day. The children had been uncooperative and extremely agitated. Even though he understood their behaviour, it had taken all his ingenuity to appease them.

As soon as he'd walked through the door, Sarah had presented him with a large envelope. It was addressed to Monsieur Hugo Rocher.

He knew exactly who it was from before he opened it. He recognised his father's handwriting. The return address was further confirmation.

Reluctant to open the envelope, he left it on the kitchen table and went outside.

Knowing he needed some alone time, she remained silent. Luckily, Nico was in his bedroom and wouldn't disturb him.

She poured a glass of white wine, walked outside and placed it on the table in front of him.

Leaving him to ponder, she went back inside to check on Nico.

With thoughts of his early childhood circling around his head, he recalled the day his father had told him that he was leaving. At the time, he'd been more angry than upset.

Although the yearly support payments had continued to be deposited in his bank account, Hugo wondered whether his father had any idea that Nicole had died.

After checking on her son, who was asleep, Sarah took the wine bottle outside and sat beside him.

Refilling his empty glass, she poured some wine into her own glass.

She couldn't find any words to say to him, so again she remained silent.

He looked at her and smiled.

"It's from my père. I can't read it yet. I'll leave it until morning."

She nodded.

Holding hands, they gazed at the sun as it sank beneath the horizon.

An unexplainable numbness had penetrated his body. Subconsciously, he knew that his père's unwelcome image would occupy the space in his mind and it would have an adverse effect on his sleep.

CHAPTER TWENTY ONE
July

He opened the envelope and dragged out a wad of paperwork and two smaller envelopes.

Four words were written on one of them; *To My Son, Hugo*. A sudden wave of nausea washed over him and he wanted to throw up. Clenching his fists, he straightened his back and sat upright in the chair, in preparation for what he was about to read.

He pushed the envelope away from him and folded his arms; trying to create a wide barrier between himself and the unwelcome stationery.

He lingered for a few moments, before picking it up again and slowly opening it. Unfolding the sheet of paper, he skimmed through the contents.

Dear Hugo

You will be reading this letter because I have passed away.

Firstly, I would like to apologise for leaving. I had to leave. It was hard for me to cope with your behaviour and your maman's illness. I know it was selfish of me and, for that, I am truly sorry.

I won't bore you with what I did with my life, other than I was extremely successful; although not very happy!

Secondly, I am bequeathing you the proceeds from the sale of my homes and my businesses; details of which are enclosed. Please make contact with my solicitor. He has been instructed to deal with the transaction.

I want you to know that I, like you, was autistic; as was your paternal grand-père. It seems that autism runs in our family, on the male side. I was only formally diagnosed when I came to America, but my symptoms were very similar to yours.

I've often thought about returning to France to meet you again. I couldn't pluck up the courage.

I hope you can forgive me.

Your Père

Devoid of any feeling at that moment, he took hold of the other envelope and tore it open.

Several photographs dropped out onto the floor. One was of himself, sat on a sun-lounger reading a book, when he was younger. Several childhood memories came flooding back, as he recalled that very moment when his father had telephoned him to say that he wouldn't be arriving; he'd had some important deal to clinch!

There were a few photographs of his father holding him when he was a baby. Hugo's facial features now, strongly resembled those of his father's, at that time he had left.

Seeing the photographs had unsettled him; his conflicting emotions making him feel unwell.

He looked towards the formal-looking will and, opening the document, he skimmed over the contents. He'd been a very wealthy man!

Far from being impressed by the contents, he felt indifferent to the information in front of him; except for the fact that he wasn't interested in accepting his money – or his apology!

He sat, in silence, contemplating his early childhood. Vivid recollections filled his head; some of which he'd rather forget. Disagreeing with his father and disliking his arrogance were there at the forefront of his recall and his reserved and dictatorial manner had been threatening. Whilst he hadn't been frightened to challenge his father, he had been scared of what might happen if his parent lost his temper.

Interrupting his solitude, Nico came and sat beside him. He'd been completely unaware that his son had been observing him from his bedroom window.

"She is there now Père, watching us."

"Who is, son?"

"A beautiful lady. She is over there. Look."

A luminous, female outline was hovering above the sculpture.

"I have seen her several times, Père. Is it Grand-mère Nicole? She talks to me before I go to sleep. I did not want to tell you. I wanted it to be a secret."

"Have you? Yes, I do believe it is. So, you have a secret, do you? Shall I tell you my secret?"

He tapped his feet and clapped his hands.

"Yes, Père."

"She comes to me too, especially when she thinks I am sad."

"Does she? When are you sad?"

"I'm not sad all the time. It's just when I miss her."

"Tell me more about her."

Hugo relayed the story about his mother exactly as it was. He also told him about the recent letter from his birth father and the will.

Later, when his son had gone inside, he thought more about how his father's absence had allowed him to forge a bond with Serge.

On an equally positive note, maybe it was meant to have happened the way it did!

As he ran his fingers through his shoulder-length hair and held his head in his hands, Sarah sat beside him. Seeking to comfort him, she spoke softly.

"Hugo, he did what he did. What happened to you is history. Try to let go of it. Holding onto it will only destroy your soul."

"I know what you're saying is right, but it still hurts."

She understood his sentiments. She too had ingested others' disapproval when she was a young girl. She'd held onto the emotional toxins for a long time. They'd left a self-destructing effect on her life.

"Amend your thoughts, Hugo. Think about what happened. You were given the opportunity to build on an already-strong and loving relationship with your maman. When she was really ill, you tended to her needs and she taught you much. You also gave Serge the opportunity to become a père to you; a role that he always yearned for. He cherishes you and loves you like you were his own son."

He bent his head to conceal his emotions. He was extremely grateful for how they'd cared for him and guided him. With their love and support, he'd grown in many different ways.

"Forgive him. Don't make him the excuse for how you feel. If you continue thinking like you do, you will continue being a victim."

She'd remembered Suzette offering her the

same advice when she was a headstrong teenager and, at that time, she'd resisted her guidance.

"Do you think you could just accept that it happened?"

He thought about what she'd said. It was painful to think about it.

"Sarah, there were so many questions that I needed answers to. I thought I'd dealt with the issues, but they're still there. He rejected me. He rejected Maman. He deserted us. We had to fend for ourselves!"

He assumed that Sarah would know how he felt. He also assumed he was ok because he hadn't spoken in depth about it – expect on the occasions when he'd had a few too many glasses of wine. He assumed that if he buried his feelings, that they wouldn't resurface and hurt him again.

"I'll work on it. I'll try."

She leant over and embraced him.

"I've made a decision. I'm going to donate some of my inheritance to the school. I'll also donate some to the people in Nepal for better health services and for the clean water project, which Eve and Gabriel are working on. Some can go towards setting up our organic food enterprise and the remainder of it will be put in trust for Nico when he's older."

Observing his reaction, a peaceful sensation penetrated her heart chakra as his words took her breath away.

His altruistic endeavour would benefit many

people and increase their quality of life. More importantly, it would have a massive impact on their education and survival.

As an holistic therapist, Sarah recognised that his actions would aid his own healing. Maybe it would help in purging himself of the harmful reactions to the rejections, which he had been nurturing for a long time.

Looking at it from a human perspective, his father's actions had caused him much anguish.

From a spiritual perspective, transformation had spontaneously occurred and his more-than-substantial inheritance would significantly reduce suffering for many people.

From the latter perspective, had his father's life been worthwhile?

He thought of the consequences of those actions. Not all of them were negative. He'd try to forgive him.

CHAPTER TWENTY TWO
August

Serge knew something wasn't right. Over the past twelve months, he'd experienced sporadic pains in his chest.

Of late, they seemed to be getting worse. His breathing had been somewhat laboured and an irritating cough had become more frequent. When he'd been out walking with Nico, he'd had some difficulty climbing up even the shortest of inclines at the side of the canal.

When alone in his studio, his inner voice had been persistently nudging him to spend more meaningful time with his wife.

They'd just eaten a light breakfast outside on the kitchen terrace. It was late August and the weather was still extremely hot; although other parts of France were experiencing heavy bouts of rainfall.

"Let's travel, Suzette. Let's go exploring."

She placed her cup onto the saucer. Always open to new experiences in her life, her husband's unexpected compulsion to travel had intrigued her.

"I'd love to, darling. What makes you want to go travelling?"

She'd noticed over the last few days that he'd been much quieter than he usually was. They respected each other's need for alone-time, so she wasn't too perturbed; although she did sense that something was troubling him!

"I just thought it'd be a change for us to do something different. Just the two of us."

His unique facial expression, reserved only for her, melted her heart. Vibrant waves of energy entered her solar plexus. She was excited!

"Where shall we go?"

"I thought we might go back to Italy; to the Tuscan region this time. We could stay in Florence and then visit Pisa and the surrounding area."

"I'd really love that. We could go to some of the museums and art galleries; and just admire the breathtaking Renaissance architecture. We could eat in some of the trattorias and visit the artisan markets."

He nodded and smiled at her again; grateful for the emotional chemistry and the love they shared. His life had been transformed since he'd met her. They'd entered into a mutual relationship where they appreciated each other's uniqueness and needs. They understood themselves and they understood each other.

The dynamics of their relationship thrived on a successful mixture of connection, compromise and companionship; closed linked to a magnetic, physical intimacy, which was both a customary and satisfying occurrence.

"Well, we can do all of that, ma chérie. I've just got some work to finish in the studio and then, when we've eaten, we can research some places to stay."

Serge cleared the table before going over to his studio, whilst Suzette gathered her gardening gloves and tools and walked over to the vegetable patch.

Whilst digging up some vegetables for their dinner, she thought of how compatible they were. Their shared awareness had enabled them to learn from each other. She couldn't imagine their lives being any other way.

Following lunch, they took their wine-filled flutes into the living area and relaxed on the sofa. Sifting through several websites, they finally chose a quiet, hamlet location within the surroundings of a medieval castle in the undulating Tuscan hills.

It was the spectacular photographs of the impressively decorated cottage and the castle that had immediately enticed them. Images of the panoramic terraces, surrounded by endless sloping vineyards and olive groves which looked like they'd been hand-painted, had provided them with all the information they needed to know.

By sheer chance, they'd managed to secure a farmworker's cottage, which was one of a group of four situated in the castle grounds.

When Serge had enquired about vacancies, he'd been informed that some wedding guests who were due to attend a wedding that weekend had cancelled. They were in luck!

Once flights had been booked and transport to the castle had been arranged, they immediately went over to inform Hugo and Sarah of the news that they would be flying to Italy in two days' time.

CHAPTER TWENTY THREE
August

Hugo and Sarah had been pleasantly surprised. Nico had grumbled; not able to understand why they wouldn't take him with them. His constant pleading had tugged at their heartstrings.

On several visits, throughout the following day, he'd repeatedly begged them to rethink their plans.

"Please take me with you Grand-père. I will be a good boy."

Serge had to delve into his inner strength to deal with his pleading.

"You're always a good boy. We'll be back very soon."

The little boy had gripped tightly onto his grand-père's leg, not wanting him to go.

Sarah had driven them to the airport. Nico had initially refused to go to school, but with much persuasion from Hugo, he'd finally agreed to go.

Settled on the rear seats of the plane, they browsed through the brochures and ordered some refreshments. As Suzette reached into her bag to pay the flight attendant, her hand felt the envelope that Nico had given to her earlier.

Placing the remainder of the loose coins into the zipped pocket of her bag, she removed the envelope and smiled; somewhat apprehensive of what would be inside.

Carefully opening the envelope, she took out a folded piece of paper and, together, they read it.

Lost for words, they gazed at each other. The connection they shared with Nico was intense. Nico's preciseness in his neatly typed letter had both pleased them and touched them at the same time.

Dear Grand-mère and Grand-père
    I do hope that you have an exciting time on your holiday.
    I am not very happy that I could not come with you.
    I am missing you already. Next time, I will come with you.
    With love and kisses from
    Nico Serge Couture xxx xxx
Oh! I forgot to say that I am sorry for being naughty.

Suzette had been teaching him computer skills and how to touch-type and his aptitude for learning was noteworthy.

Whilst being conscious of not interfering in Nico's upbringing, they were thankful to have been given the chance to have some influence on his life.

She remembered how thankful she'd been for her own father's influence on her two children. He'd looked after them, when she'd been a single parent and needed to work. His gentleness and his quirky sense of humour had rubbed off on them.

Carefully folding the letter, she put it back inside the envelope and placed it within the zipped pocket of her handbag for safekeeping!

"You *will* find your way in life, Nico. You will", she whispered to herself.

CHAPTER TWENTY FOUR
September

The taxi driver confidently steered his trusty old cab around the hairpin bends, on the steep ascent towards the hilltop castle dominating the Tuscan landscape.

Following their stifling plane journey, they welcomed the fragrant essences of the wild herbs and flowers which filtered through the cab's open windows.

They were jolted in their seats as the driver pressed his brakes as they came to a sharp halt, in front of the grand castle entrance.

Mirroring each other, they both raised their eyebrows and pursed their lips, as they watched the driver hurriedly retrieve their luggage from the boot and drag their cases up a short flight of steps through the castle doorway.

Without comment, they stepped out into the heat and stood still for a few moments, soaking in the 360° panoramic views. Amazed at the natural beauty of the rolling hills, abundant with olive groves and endless rows of vines, they knowingly nodded at each other.

After paying the anxious driver, who was most likely in a hurry to capture his next fare, they went up the steps and entered the castle.

The breathtaking décor in the reception area took them by surprise. Several large Renaissance paintings adorned the walls and luxurious pieces of Italian, antique chairs and sofas were positioned around the expansive area.

Suzette was scrutinising the portrait of a young man dressed in period costume, whilst Serge was moseying around, admiring the carefully restored features of the ancient architecture. Intrigued by the ornate carvings which took pride of place over the top and side of a wide fireplace, he stopped to examine them further.

His eyes were on stalks as he walked over to two grey pillars, which stood sentinel at each side of the heavily-carved reception desk. Letting his hand rest gently on one of the cool marble pillars, a shiver ran up his spine as he inspected several unique fracture lines sprawling up to the top of the pillar. He imagined how challenging it would have been, all those years ago, to transport the colossal marble pillars up the mountainside. No doubt they'd have employed a sizeable team of strong men, controlling numerous wooden sledges with strong ropes, to haul them up to the castle.

In a corner, by a large stairway, Suzette had detected how the artist had cleverly captured the extreme sadness in the young man's doleful eyes. She wondered what he might have been thinking, whilst the artist daubed his paint on the canvas.

They were interrupted from their ponderings by footsteps on the stone floor.

"Buongiorno Sig. E Sig.ra Couture. Benvenuti nel nostro castello."

An elegant lady came from out of a room behind the reception desk. Little did they both know, that she had been observing them surveying her home. She wanted to witness their reaction and she'd been pleased with what she'd seen. Almost all of the people who came to stay, were amazed by the impressive renovation of the ancient castle and its surroundings.

"Buongiorno Signora", they both replied.

"Do you speak English?"

Suzette nodded.

"I'm Signora Firenze, but you can call me Maria. I'm English by birth and came to Italy over forty years ago. I met my husband on holiday in Florence and married him soon after."

"I'm English too. I met my husband, Serge, in France and now I live there with him."

He nodded and smiled, acknowledging the obvious commonality between the two women.

Following a fascinating documentary about the castle's heritage and the mammoth restoration project, Maria escorted them outside and along a descending path to the cottage where they'd be staying.

Before handing them the keys, Maria offered some information about the wedding which would be taking place on Friday.

"Oh! I forget to tell you. The bride and groom have invited you to their wedding. They'd also like you to join them for aperitivo later at 7.00 in the courtyard. You'll be able to meet the other guests."

Serge's phone rang. It was Nico.

Maria waved as she left.

"I'll be there as well. See you later."

CHAPTER TWENTY FIVE
September

Already inebriated with the amount of Italian wine they'd drank at the pre-wedding gathering, they were now even more inebriated with the sensory overload of the multihued Tuscan landscape, which was slowly changing before their eyes.

Snuggling closely, they gazed into the horizon as the abstract edges of the silvery sun against a golden backdrop, disappeared behind a range of mountains.

The relaxing sounds of the crickets kept them company as they sipped on more wine, which had been included in the complimentary hamper of foodstuffs on their arrival.

Picturesque Italy had a similar feel to France with its abundant vegetation, vivid greenery and vibrant landscapes; not forgetting the climate.

In the far-off distance they could see lights twinkling in the clusters of cottages and the tall spire of a church steeple.

From where they were relaxing, on the vast secluded terrace, the panorama had a magical feel about it.

"I feel so honoured to have been invited to the wedding, Serge."

Smiling, he gripped her hand.

Lifting their wine flutes, they toasted each other's health before taking a sip of the crisp, Vernaccia di San Gimignano wine. The young, straw coloured blend was different to the wines they usually drank. It was a much drier blend, but their palates soon adapted to the unusual, lingering bitter aftertaste of pears, apples and almonds.

With senses stirring, they held each other's gaze, playfully teasing one another with knowing thoughts.

She loved the way he touched his lips when he was deep in thought. She loved the way his steel-grey, wavy hair touched his collar. She loved the intoxicating smell of his manliness and his sensual touch.

The sound of his voice when he spoke to her and sang some of her favourite songs, would send rigid shivers of passion down the length of her spine.

When he danced with her, he could easily have been mistaken for a professional dancer as he waltzed her around the living area in their home.

She loved the way he tapped his fingers and his feet when any kind of music was playing. His natural musicality was undeniably potent when he played the piano. Nico had learnt that same habit of holding his hand to his mouth, from him.

In fact, she loved everything about him!

As she ran her fingers through his hair, a pulsating sensation in her sacral region alerted her to her craving for him.

He leant over and kissed her; gently at first and then with an increasing passion. The taste of his lips left her wanting more.

His hands began to explore almost every part of her near-naked body. She never tired of his touch!

Appreciating his attention, she anticipated what was to come. Her desire heightened and a euphoric thrumming inside her head made her feel shaky.

Usually, their partaking in lovemaking was of equal contribution. However, on this occasion, he unselfishly pleasured her, without considering his own sensual longing.

Mesmerised by her curvaceous beauty, he kissed her again, gently this time.

Sensing her ever growing need, the intense magnetism of their love drew them closer towards each other and he lavished even more attention on her.

With sexual energy intensifying, he finally

surrendered to her unspoken pleas and his own pressing desire.

Simultaneously, in intimate embrace, they moved rhythmically and frenziedly under the stars; sealing their love for each other.

CHAPTER TWENTY SIX
September

The familiar WhatsApp ringtone alerted them to Nico's call. His excited face appeared on the screen, and it made him smile.

"Bonjour Grand-père. Are you both having a wonderful time over there?"

Suzette joined her husband on the terrace.

"Bonjour, Nico. Yes, we are. We're going to a wedding today. How are you?"

"Grand-père, are you not already married to Grand-mère?"

Both laughed at their grandson's reply.

"Yes. I am. We're going to someone else's wedding in a castle."

In a real castle? What is it like? Will you send me some photographs please?"

"We will. Is everything ok at home?"

"Oui. We have been doing some gardening and cooking. Grand-mère, I have baked some of your favourite lemon and lime madeleines. If you were here, you could eat them with me."

Chuckling, she thought of how she'd taught him to bake and how he'd followed her recipe to the smallest detail; perfecting the scallop shaped cakes, so that they were brown and crispy on the outside and spongy on the inside. She liked them dipped with milk chocolate, but Nico preferred them with just a dusting of granulated sugar.

"Grand-père, I have been working on a new piece of music."

"Magnifique. You can play for me when we come home. We'll email you some photos, but we need to get ready now for the wedding. Au revoir. Keep working on your music."

The little boy blew kisses, before the screen went blank.

Serge pictured his grandson's small fingers caressing the black and white keys of his piano; every single note so subtle and deliberate. His ongoing obsession with perfecting his technique was part of his autism. He had to practice every day or else he'd become agitated. Routine was so important to him.

They quickly dressed and walked, hand in hand, along the winding path up to the castle.

She turned to him, admiring his casual, yet distinct style. He'd chosen to wear his navy and white striped, linen shirt with some white linen trousers, rolled up at the hem and some white leather loafers.

Her thrown-together ensemble consisted of a brightly-coloured shift dress and a yellow scarf, tied loosely around her head.

Nestled within the 18th century castle walls, in the chapel, the guests waited for the bride to arrive. The local Catholic priest was speaking to the groom as they sneaked in and sat on the back pews. The bride and groom, who had been legally married in England before they came, were going to have a nuptial mass.

At precisely 2.00pm the organist began to play Wagner's Bridal March to announce the bride's entrance. As she waited inside the chapel door, the tall white candles on either side of the altar, created flickering shadows on the ancient stone walls.

Escorted by her father, she walked slowly down the centre aisle, her white lace shift dress hung closely to her sylph frame and her high-heels tapped on the tiled floor as she moved forward towards her waiting groom. She held a small posy of white roses and several strands of gypsophila were threaded through her long dark hair which trailed down towards her waist.

Throwing convention to the wind, the bridesmaids also wore white mid-length satin dresses with silver-leaf headbands in their hair. It was an all-white wedding; even the groom and best man wore white linen suits.

During the ceremony, the married guests were invited to renew their wedding vows and the priest gave a blessing to all of the wedding party.

Suzette and Serge also renewed their vows and they stood with the others, throwing white rose petals over the newly-weds as they walked through the chapel entrance.

After endless amounts of photographs had been taken, the guests mingled around the castle courtyard, drinking Prosecco cocktails as they waited to welcome the bride and groom.

Waiters strolled around, serving a selection of appetising canapes, consisting of Parmigiano cheese flakes with salted almonds, rough chunks of bruschetta thinly smeared with basil and sundried tomatoes, stuffed olives and cinnamon cheese cubes; whilst Italian classical music echoed down into the valley beyond the castle.

Within the coolness of the banqueting hall, cascading flower arrangements adorned the walls and the ceilings and tables were minimally dressed with narrow garlands of eucalyptus leaves and white rose centrepieces.

With everyone seated, the wedding feast commenced at exactly 5.00pm. The heightened buzz of animated conversation and the loud howls of laughter were sure signs that the celebration was off to a good start. Suzette was pleased to hear the familiar Liverpool accent of the people who were sat on the table with her and Serge.

Whilst the hungry guests tucked into the first course, which consisted of vegetarian ravioli or mini tomato and herb meatballs, a magician circulated between the tables, entertaining the children and adults alike.

As the second course of lemon, lime and mint sorbetto was being served, one of the waiters burst into song, singing 'What would I do without your smile now?' Silence flooded the space and emotions flowed freely as he serenaded the couple with several choruses of 'All of Me'. It was their special song.

Following a rousing applause, the main course of seared sea bass with rosemary potatoes and porcini mushrooms or eggplant and scallion flan with roasted vegetables, was served.

After several, lengthy speeches, the bride and groom cut the top layer of the three-tiered wedding cake, which consisted of a dark Belgian chocolate cake filled with vanilla buttercream, a lemon coconut cake filled with a zesty lemon curd and buttercream frosting and an apricot-infused sponge, filled with marbled buttercream.

Wanting the guests to enjoy their wedding cake with them, they decided to serve the cake as the dessert.

Later, as the sun set, the guests danced the night away to a live band.

As Suzette gazed into her husband's sleepy eyes, she propositioned him.

"As we've renewed our wedding vows, does

this mean we can have a second honeymoon?"

He raised his eyebrows and grinned.

"Madame Couture. I thought we were on a permanent honeymoon!"

CHAPTER TWENTY SEVEN
September

During the remainder of their holiday, they strolled around the grounds of the castle or just lazed on the terrace, enjoying the clean air and the idyllic countryside. Suzette was engrossed in a new novel whilst Serge sketched numerous designs for some new carvings. Other days, they'd go sight-seeing.

Nico facetimed every day, wanting to know every single detail of what they'd been doing.

Although post wedding activities and visits had been arranged for the guests, they declined offers, preferring to explore the area on their own.

One day they took a taxi to the train station and boarded the train into Florence. Eating gelatos and crunching on toasted coconut macarons, they meandered in and out of the cobbled back streets, visiting several museums and ancient cathedrals, admiring the spectacular architecture and art.

On other days, they hopped on and off the train, visiting Montepulciano and Pisa, where they bought gifts for themselves and their family.

On a visit to the Battistero di San Giovanti in Florence, Serge became fascinated with Donatello's classical carvings inside of the religious building.

Although the sculptor's style was in total contrast to his own, he fully appreciated how Donatello had cleverly captured the spirit of the Renaissance era.

He recalled how he'd studied Donatello at University and how his dissertation had included details of the sculptor's naturalistic statue of David with its enigmatic smile. It had been implied that Donatello was expressing his own sexual attitudes through this creation, which was a risky thing to do in the 1440's.

As he slumped down on a pew in front of one of the statues, Suzette's silent concern for her husband nagged at her. Over the past few days, his lack of energy and his constant need to rest was disturbing. She couldn't understand it, when he was usually so fit.

His over-attentiveness, more so than his usual thoughtfulness, also alerted her.

Seeing her watching him, he altered his posture and winked. Her heart skipped several beats as she pushed her negative thoughts away; not wanting her intuition to guide her along an unwelcome path. Nevertheless, the gut feeling stayed with her for the remainder of the holiday.

CHAPTER TWENTY EIGHT
September

On their return from Italy, Suzette had persuaded him to see Gilbert, his doctor. She'd noticed that he'd been coughing up small globules of blood and was tiring more.

In his effort to reassure her, he'd told her that he thought it was only a slight chest infection.

Her sixth sense had warned her to the fact that it could be something more serious.

After examining him, Gilbert had taken a blood sample, to be forwarded to the hospital for analysis. So certain was he, that Serge's indicators were sinister, he'd immediately telephoned to make appointments for him to attend for x-rays and a body scan at the local hospital.

He'd also telephoned the senior oncologist for

an urgent appointment for the following week.

Serge's weight loss and his chronic coughing and shortness of breath, coupled with the rusty-coloured phlegm that he'd been coughing up, had alarmed him. He was more than certain that the prolonged exposure to silica dust had contributed to his patient's symptoms.

From a professional stance, Gilbert was in a quandary; especially if his prognosis was accurate.

The sensitive situation was tough to deal with. He'd been Serge's GP for a long time and had, over the years, developed a close friendship with him and his family.

As Suzette and Serge left the consulting room, he hugged them both, silently hoping that his professional prediction would be proved wrong.

CHAPTER TWENTY NINE
September

Waiting for the results was torture. Cocooned in their own world, they visited the labyrinth twice daily within the clearing that he'd created. They went there, not only to meditate, but to try and process their own thoughts.

Holding hands in the summer house, they sat in silence. Talking about it would deepen the fears they both had.

She tried to remain positive for him and sensing his fear, she channelled all her energy into him.

He tried to remain positive for her, but the niggling feeling in the pit of his stomach, continued to convince him that the outcome he was waiting for, wouldn't be what he wanted to hear.

They hadn't heard Nico arrive. He popped his head through the door and peered in.

"I have been looking for you. I want to tell you all about what I have been doing in school. I want to tell you about Autumn."

Suzette smiled as climbed onto the seat at the side of Serge.

"Have you, darling? We were just having a quiet moment."

Immediately sensing their low moods, he knew something was wrong.

"Grand-père. Are you feeling poorly? Do you need some medicine? Your face is different."

"No. I'm not poorly. Just a little tired."

"Oh! I came to ask if we could go for a walk along the canal and collect some leaves. We are doing a project at school."

"I'm not that tired that I can't take a walk with you, Nico and when we get back, you can play your new piece of music for me."

Spending some time with him would take his mind off the impending results. His grandson always seemed to turn up at an appropriate time.

The three of them walked back to the house and whilst Serge and Nico picked up a paper bag to collect the leaves, she gathered her cleaning stuff and set about cleaning every surface in the house.

CHAPTER THIRTY
September

They sat in the tense-filled waiting room at the hospital, holding hands and desperately waiting for the consultant to invite them into his consulting room.

Suzette was anxious, frightened and numb, not wanting to hear what she suspected; wanting to hear that everything would be fine.

Serge sat quietly and waited patiently.

"Come in please, Monsieur Couture. You too, Madame."

The consultant oncologist calmly explained that the x-rays and scans had revealed lung cancer. It had reached a stage where it was inoperable.

Waiting for a moment for the devastating news to register, he looked towards the nurse to offer further support. It was never an easy task informing someone of their results, especially when the diagnosis was terminal.

The room started to spin as Suzette grasped her husband's hand tightly. A stabbing pain seared through her chest. Her hands and body began to shudder uncontrollably as the consultant gave his diagnosis. She could hardly catch her breath as the nurse moved closer and firmly rested a hand on her shoulder.

"The type of cancer you have, has been a slow-growing one. Your doctor has suggested that the silica dust from your work may have caused the damage. It has. The silica has invaded your lungs and has become trapped in your lung tissue."

He fully understood that the damage to his health, was related to his occupation.

The silence was palpable as it flooded the room.

"You understand what I'm saying, Serge?"

He lowered his head and nodded. Even though he'd had an inkling, he hadn't really been prepared for the diagnosis.

"I'd suspected it would be cancer. Thank you for telling me. How long do I have?"

"It's not possible for me to give you an accurate prognosis. If I say three months, I may not be correct. Some of my patients have lived longer than my prognostication. The nurse will advise you on the different forms of medication that will help you with your breathing difficulties."

The consultant waited for a few minutes before standing up. He didn't want to appear as if he was rushing his patient out of the room, but his next patient was waiting. He would have to deliver the same devastating result to him. Although he'd undergone training on how to deal with these unfortunate events, it didn't become any easier. He wished he'd been taught much more at medical school, on how to effectively deal with his own emotions when having to explain critical news to his patients.

Feeling burnt-out and dispirited; he suddenly became aware that he needed to take some time out and evaluate his own psychological health.

He wanted to sit with his patient and hold his hand. The scared expression in Serge's eyes bore into his own. He wanted to explain more about the disease and ways to try and accept the life-changing news. Once more, he questioned his choice of career. He acknowledged that he was an outstanding surgeon with a genuine desire to heal, but his countless patient successes didn't satisfy his desire to do more to work on improving the mental health issues that came with terminal diagnosis. His decision was made. He was going to book himself into a retreat and take some time from from his demanding practice, to honestly re-evaluate his life. Unknowingly to Serge, his patient's visit had been a catalyst for change.

Thanking the consultant, Serge also stood up. The stark reality of what he'd been told hadn't registered at first, but now he wanted to get away from the hospital as fast as he could.

The nurse guided them into a side room and explained that chemotherapy wouldn't have any effect at this late stage. She'd arrange for him to have palliative care during the final stages of his illness and a counselling service would be provided, if they required it.

Suzette could hardly believe what she was hearing. Palliative care! If he needed any palliative care, she'd be the one to provide it.

She turned towards her husband; his dignity and bravery visibly exposed on his face. She fought, without success, to prevent her tears escaping.

As they left the hospital, he clutched onto her hand tightly. He didn't have the energy to get behind the wheel and drive home.

"We know that human life isn't forever, Suzette."

She knew that there were no guarantees in life, except death; but contemplating the future without her husband, was something she definitely did not choose to deliberate on.

Unconsciously competent, she drove home, with the consultant's prognosis and Serge's words echoing loudly inside her head.

CHAPTER THIRTY ONE
September

Following the shock of his diagnosis, they'd lived in a protected vacuum for the first few days; trying to come to terms with the inevitable, before breaking the news to their family and friends.

Although she wanted him to herself, she recognised that others would want to spend some valuable time with him too. It was critical to everyone's wellbeing.

On the days when Serge felt well enough, family visits were frequent. Suzette's children and her grandchildren had travelled over and stayed with them for seven days. As was per usual before his diagnosis, Hugo, Sarah and Nico would drop in each day to check on them.

One Monday evening, with just a laptop and

several glasses of Limoux for company, they researched art galleries around the Aude province.

The following Wednesday afternoon, after lunch, they drove along the A61 road to the hilltop village of Fanjeaux. Several internet reviews had reported the village as being uninspiring. They didn't agree. As they strolled around the former convent of the Dominicans and the Monastery of Notre Dame de Prouilhe, they were fascinated with the history of the place.

They meandered over to Maison Gramont, where numerous pieces of contemporary art were being exhibited. As the doors opened at 3.30pm, they were the first to enter.

Individually, they wandered off, browsing and scrutinising a plethora of abstract paintings, sculptures, ceramics, drawings and textiles - all of which were to their taste.

Later, whilst sitting outside in the shaded courtyard, drinking freshly squeezed orange, they nibbled at some pastries and discussed the pieces they'd admired.

After a twelve minute drive along the D623, they arrived at the beautiful village of Cambrieure. Luckily the Kinetic Art Gallery was open until seven o'clock and so they spent another hour, observing the eclectic pieces of moving art created by the engineering genius, Jean Francois Scalbert.

Totally engrossed in the multi-dimensional movements of the exhibits, Suzette was intrigued to discover that Scalbert had been born in the same year as her – 1953. She perused over written excerpts from artistic periods in his life, admiring his enthusiasm for exploring fresh and diverse techniques. Smiling, she compared her own piece of engineering genius, Oscillate, to his shifting pieces of art.

His work had evoked emotions in her and she felt motivated to complete more kinetic pieces.

Serge had been discreetly watching her, as he feigned inspection of a rotating structure which simulated human body movements. He loved and admired everything about her.

With her help, he'd been trying to live his life as near as it was possible to how it was before his diagnosis, but the shock of it was hard for them both to accept. They didn't pretend that everything would be ok. Both understood that it was a case of 'when', not 'if'.

As she walked over to where he was sitting, she could see that the colour had drained from his face. The outing had been too much for him.

As they drove home, with Suzette at the wheel chattering about Scalbert's work, she wasn't surprised as she glanced over to see that he'd fallen asleep at the side of her. He was exhausted!

Later that evening, they joined together. Their love, physical as it was, was not just a purely sexual act; it was profoundly spiritual. In complete harmony, they moved simultaneously in a gentler embrace than their usual intimate encounters.

As he held her close, his humour was still in

existence as he struggled with his breathing.

"It's you, Suzette. You take my breath away every time I'm near you."

Her smile didn't mask her pain.

Gazing at her, he identified with her angst.

They'd both agreed to be entirely honest with each other; no hiding of feelings, no untruths.

"Suffering is relative, ma chérie. It opens the heart. Every one of us suffers in different ways. I know that we're both openly emotional and are able to cry easily, but there are others who suffer internally without displaying tears."

She squeezed his hand.

"Hugo is in denial, Suzette. He's adamant that I'm going to recover."

Words were absent, as she lay in his arms.

In wanting things to remain as normal as possible, he was determined that he'd continue to drive, sculpt and spend time with Hugo and Nico.

The overwhelming, emotional impact of what was happening, had brought all of his family more closer than they were before.

CHAPTER THIRTY TWO
November

The day had finally arrived. Organising the event had been a mammoth task. With much help, Hugo had managed to complete the scheduling of the event in time.

Parents, employers who'd been involved in the project and some representatives from educational establishments, were invited to witness the success of every child.

Students who'd left the school the previous term, had also been invited.

The visitors began arriving at 2.30pm.

Far from things going to plan, chaos reigned.

Some children refused to participate. Not familiar with there being with so many strangers in the school, they became agitated.

The visitors entering the school hall, were unaware that the welcoming music was being provided by Nico. It was only when they saw him at the side of the stage that they realised that the music was live.

At 3pm precisely, the principal welcomed everyone, explaining how the implementation of the project and innovative teaching methods had contributed to the children's achievement levels.

As part of their differentiated learning, the children had formed a choir. Diligently, they'd been practicing daily.

Accompanied by reassuring teachers, the younger children were brought to the front of the audience. One boy was crying and didn't want to sing. He was quickly taken back to his mother, who comforted him and took him outside.

Nico, who was already seated at the piano, began to play. The nervous children, who'd been rehearsing for several weeks, stood upright and sang their hearts out. After taking a bow, they returned to their seats.

Loud applause from the audience echoed throughout the school hall. Two more children were overwhelmed and had to be taken out of the hall. The noise was unbearable for them. After being given headphones to wear, to block out the noise, they went back to the hall.

Hugo took hold of the microphone and thanked the audience, explaining that some of the children were hypersensitive to noise. He asked the audience to kindly express their appreciation by waving their hands.

Once all the certificates had been presented by Gilbert Guerisseur, Pierre delivered a short speech about his experiences since leaving school. Although his confidence had improved, he was still nervous as he walked to the front of the audience.

He relayed how his employer had noticed his keen eye for detail and his skill for developing new flavours in his baking. His strict work ethos and his passion for pastry had led to him being trained alongside one of France's prestigious pastry chefs.

He'd also won several 'Employee of the Month' accolades for his dedication to his work.

The audience waved their hands to applaud him, although some did forget and clapped loudly. Pierre nodded in acknowledgement and introduced Nico, before leaving the stage.

The little boy walked towards the front of the stage and, speaking firstly in French and then in formal English, politely thanked the audience for attending. Enlightening them about how some of the children had written poetry, he explained that they'd included their poems in a book and that the books were being sold, to raise funds for the school.

Hugo had been scanning the hall, avidly observing the audience's response to his son's introduction.

An expression of juxtaposed awe and disbelief swept through the audience as eyebrows were raised. Mouths gaped wide, as they hung onto his son's every word. Looking over to where his family were sitting in the audience, he nodded.

Unbeknown to Hugo, Gilbert had invited some journalists to attend. His intention was to give kudos to his and the school's efforts, in raising awareness of autism at a national and international level; more importantly he wanted to publicise how success could be achieved with differentiated teaching methods.

Hugo noticed that one journalist appeared exasperated by Nico's articulation.

"I thought he was French. Why does he speak in that snooty, upper-class English accent? He sounds geeky; so old for his age."

Another journalist answered him with her own question.

"Someone said he was autistic. How can he be, if he plays the piano like that? He's only a child. I thought they weren't supposed to be able to do normal things."

Sarah, who was sitting near them, heard their narrow-minded comments. She stiffened her body and clenched her teeth. It was her son that they were talking about! How dare they! The blinkered bastards!

She was on the verge of reproaching them, when she noticed Nico checking that the others were stood exactly in line. Initially, persuading the children to recite their poems had been difficult and some of them were already tapping their feet and wringing their hands, ready to flee.

One boy started screaming. There was too much activity going on in the room and he was frightened. He didn't want to read his poem.

Sarah walked over to him and comforted him. With some gentle persuasion, he took his place on the stage with the other children and one little girl held his hand.

She smiled as she watched her son fixate on making sure that everything was as it should be. His persistent penchant for perfection could be annoying, but she found it entertaining to watch, as Nico scanned the audience and waited patiently for them to be silent.

She recollected how Suzette had previously encouraged Nico to write down exactly what he felt about being autistic.

He'd spent a great amount of time, jotting down words and repeating them on several pieces of paper. She had then explained some of the alternative words, which could be used in his writing.

His thirst for knowledge was unquenchable and he'd proudly decided to include the newfound words in his poem.

Without need for a script, he confidently recited his poem, firstly in his mother-tongue and then in his formal English tone.

Sarah allowed her emotions to trickle down her cheeks, as Nico clearly enunciated his moral message through each line of his poem.

Nico's Wish

I see the world differently from you
I am different. You are different too

You do not understand me
I do not understand you

I misunderstand your behaviour, your words
You label me

You think I am disruptive and impolite
You become annoyed

You disregard me, exclude me
You do not try to accept me

Am I any less equal than you?

I do not need social acceptance from you
Neither will I disguise my autism for you

It is part of who I am

My autism is my advantage
Not my detriment

My wish is for understanding and
Equal values for all human beings

Can we all just learn to accept our differences?

Nico waited for the audience to wave their hands in appreciation, before he introduced the rest of the group.

Bravely, each child took their turn, peering nervously into the audience before reading from their scripts. Several of the children stammered and stumbled on their words. They improvised by inserting other words. It didn't matter. The main thing was that they were contributing and the audience were waving their hands frantically in approval of their efforts.

It was a proud moment for everyone.

Parents were amazed at how quickly their children's behaviour had been transformed, within the short period of time they'd been attending the school.

Hugo then invited the audience to partake of some light refreshments, whilst also reminding them to purchase the children's book of poetry.

To end the celebration, Nico delivered yet another impressive piano recital to the captivated audience.

That evening, the school in Lezignan had, undeniably, been 'put on the map'. Local radio broadcasters and national television stations were reporting how the lives of children within the locality had been transformed. The ethos within the school had been recognised as a contributory factor to their success.

Inspirational articles had been published in regional and national newspapers, with prominent front page exposure being given to the exceptional musical aptitude of a young boy who could play complex pieces of music without any printed form; as well as writing thought-provoking poetry!

Nico had achieved acclaim before he was six years old.

The local education representative, who'd been in attendance, had immediately reported his key findings to the French president's educational adviser. The president had expressed an interest in paying a visit to the school to check on their model of education.

The school envisaged that an increased understanding of autism would now be generated throughout the education system. Possibly, some of their distinctive teaching methods could be replicated throughout the country.

Awareness was long overdue!

With the expressed interest of the new president, the school anticipated the provision of further funding, which would allow them to accept a new intake of children. It would also help in securing more experienced teachers, who'd been specifically trained in methods used to address learning differences.

Later that evening, as he sat in the living room with Sarah, Hugo's thoughts went to his maman. She'd be so pleased that he and Nico had been instrumental in raising awareness of autism.

He remembered how most of his teachers had said that he wouldn't amount to much; even though they considered him to be high-functioning.

He also remembered the only teacher who had truly understood him. He wondered if that teacher, who'd believed in him, knew how much of an influence he'd been - and if he'd been watching the evening news!

CHAPTER THIRTY THREE
November

News of the young maestro's musical talent had filtered through to the critically-acclaimed, Italian composer, Barto Briziano. With no time to waste, he'd personally contacted the school, to enquire about the child virtuoso.

After a lengthy conversation with Madame Moreau, he'd requested a meeting with Nico and his parents. Firstly, he wanted to see and hear the young boy's performance and secondly, if he was as good as the press had reported, he'd offer to take him under his wing.

When Hugo and Sarah had learnt about the telephone call, they'd been wary of his motives. Having read about how several child geniuses had been exploited and pressurised to outrival others, their intensive research had revealed that Briziano insisted on absolute excellence. He had overly-high expectations of his protégés.

Nevertheless, they were also intrigued and a meeting was arranged.

On the morning of the meeting, Nico had woken at the usual time. Following his ritual of eating the same breakfast, he'd dressed himself in his habitual, sequential order.

Thankfully for Sarah, the journey to school had been uneventful.

To allow him privacy, to perform his music for the composer without interruption, the children had been taken out of school on a nature trail.

In his inimitable manner, the young maestro introduced himself.

"Bonjour, Monsieur Briziano. My name is Nico Serge Couture. I am pleased to meet you. My père informs me that you would like to hear me play. Shall I play for you now?"

Briziano nodded.

"Yes. Off you go."

He positioned himself comfortably in front of the piano. Expertly caressing the keys, his small fingertips moved effortlessly and flexibly, initially playing his own compositions without any sheet music. Next, he delivered his own renditions of Claude Debussy's Serenade of the Doll and Jimbo's Lullaby.

Briziano gave his verdict.

"Well, Nico. What can I say? I'm enormously

impressed with your skills. Have you had any professional guidance?"

He shook his head.

"My Grand-père sat me at his piano when I was three years old. I have played every day since then."

"Is your Grand-père a professional pianist?"

"No, but he is a brilliant musician."

Turning towards Hugo and Sarah, Briziano enthused again.

"Your son has such a superlative talent. He is by far the best child pianist I've heard in a long time. His attention to harmony is nothing short of remarkable and he has an ability to transmit his emotions into the compositions; capturing the mood and tempo superbly."

Hugo squeezed Sarah's hand.

"The way in which he experiments with the melodies is out of this world. If you agree, I can make him famous. Audiences throughout the world will venerate him. He will have his own orchestra and he can command his own fee."

Hugo's parental instinct went into overdrive. He didn't want his son to chase fame. Neither did he like the manner in which Briziano assumed that it was what his son would want to do.

"Let me hear you play again, Nico."

Obediently, his fingers expertly produced a piece of Briziano's own music. He'd memorised the ten minute composition, with over one thousand notes, only a few days before.

With mouth agape and his eyes closed, the composer moved his hands rhythmically from side to side. Having composed his own music at the age of eight, he was astounded by the boy's expertise.

Standing up, Nico took a bow.

"Bravo. Bravo. Perfezionare. May I ask you where you get your inspiration from?"

"I hear music in everything; in my dreams and in the countryside outside my bedroom window. I hear melodies in conversations. Some accents have a rhythm, which I can quite easily transfer into my compositions. I compose music to the sound of my maman's beautiful voice."

Her heart flipped several times at his candid admission.

"My Grand-père plays music from the 1960's and we perform duets. Music is an important part of me. I must play the piano every day, or else I am sad."

Briziano felt sure he could persuade the boy's parents to agree to him progressing their young child's already-exceptional talent. Detecting their apprehension, he recognised that he'd better not push too hard.

"So, what do you think, Nico? Would you like to come to Italy and I'll teach you how to become one the best pianists in the world? It will be a great opportunity for you."

The expressions on Hugo and Sarah's faces gave him the answer he didn't want to hear. They were far from enamoured with his offer. It wasn't something they'd envisaged for their son.

Nico had been approached several times to play in concerts in Narbonne, Carcassonne and Girona. He'd refused. He played music for his own pleasure and for his family. On rare occasions, he'd performed at local events, to raise money for charity, but that was as far as it went.

"With great respect, Monsiour Briziano, I do not wish to live in Italy. Neither do I wish to play with an orchestra. I do not want to be famous."

Surprised and irritated by Nico's reply, he tried again to persuade him.

"You will never get this opportunity again, young man."

Disliking Briziano's persistent arrogance, Hugo interrupted.

"Thank you for coming to listen to my son. He is still a young child and we don't wish to allow any pressure to be put on him."

Briziano altered his stance and his tone.

"This is one decision you will surely regret."

Muttering several profanities, he turned his back on them, picked up his file and stormed out of the room.

CHAPTER THIRTY FOUR
Seven months later – April 2019

Following a relaxed morning of sketching in his studio, Serge decided he'd like to pay a visit to the Modern Art Museum in Collioure.

He'd eaten some bread and a small bowl of soup, before he and Suzette made the journey. His taste buds weren't the same since the cancer had invaded his body.

They parked the car and strolled up the hill towards the museum. Climbing the steps to the entrance had been challenging. Breathless and stopping a few times, he was determined to reach the top. He always felt a degree of contentment in this dynamic, artistic space.

As they walked towards his sculptures, he was delighted to see some visitors critiquing his work.

They seemed impressed with the reclining carving and the smaller, more recent ones which he'd created the previous year.

He listened intently to their comments but decided against introducing himself.

After discussions with Suzette, he would donate the larger sculptures to the museum, once he'd passed away. He'd like them to be a part of his legacy which lived on in Collioure amongst the legacies of Matisse, Picasso, Pignon and Derain. The smaller carvings would be returned to his home; for members of his family.

On leaving the museum they strolled, arm-in-arm past Les Templiers bar and mingled with the holidaymakers and residents in the cobbled back streets; all of whom were enjoying the ambience of the area and totally oblivious of Serge's illness.

On occasions, in his subconscious mind, he imagined he was watching himself in a movie, with an ending he didn't want to see. He visualised himself being seized and rapidly carried along by enormous, undulating waves. He didn't have the energy to ride the tides and get back to the shore.

At other times, his unsettled mind would convince him that his cancer was heavily tattooed across his forehead for all to see. He was thankful they were oblivious! Sympathy would serve no purpose. He needed to work through it himself.

Spending time with his wife was even more important now, than it had ever been.

Sitting outside at the tables of a restaurant,

facing the 12th Century Templar castle, they both picked at their early evening meal of sea bass and fresh vegetables, before strolling over to the car park.

Before driving home, they purchased some nougat for Nico. He loved the one with meringue and raspberries.

Whilst Suzette drove, Serge soaked in the magnificent landscape, with its organic vegetation and sprawling, hillside vines. Interspersed within the countryside, were numerous apartment blocks and contemporary architectural dwellings; all of which he hadn't noticed before.

He opened the car window and gazed out towards the horizon. Even though the lavender was not yet in full bloom, the aroma permeated his nostrils. The plethora of colours in the distance, stimulated his emotions and his low mood lifted. He fully understood why artists flocked to the area to paint.

He contemplated on how the immediacy of his terminal illness had somehow heightened his already-receptive senses.

CHAPTER THIRTY FIVE
May

Intensely aware of his own impending demise, he was determined to finish his latest carving, which depicted himself and Suzette in a reclining position. It was just one of several designs he'd sketched, when they had been relaxing on the terrace in Florence.

The darker marble depicted himself and the lighter marble depicted his wife, leaning on him.

The sculpture would have a dual purpose. It would serve as a seat where his wife could rest after gardening. It would also serve as a reminder of the love they'd shared.

Although fatigue had chosen to befriend him since his diagnosis, his determination hadn't faltered. He'd work on it until it was finished. It would be his final gift to his wife.

He spoke lovingly to the piece of art as he smoothed the curved angles with sandpaper.

"Your curves will be the comfort that my wife will seek when I'm gone. She'll feel the love I've put into carving you. Take care of her for me."

He'd already chosen a location for it, just underneath the fig trees, alongside the pebbled stream.

Over the last few months, his driving force was to live long enough to spend as much time with his wife and family. He'd been relaying his family history to Nico, who'd been fascinated with what he'd heard. He'd also taught him about the Languedoc history and how the Cathars came to the region in the 12th century.

Adjusting his safety mask, he swigged some water from his flask before fixing it back in place over his face. Perhaps, if he'd worn some safety equipment in his younger days, he wouldn't have contracted the lung cancer. It was too late now!

His mind wandered to the final moments of his first wife's passing. He allowed himself to once again feel the intense pain of losing Francesca, knowing that Suzette would experience that same intenseness when he left her.

He bore no disloyalty when remembering his love for Francesca. She'd been a large part of his life and he knew that she'd visited Suzette in spirit on many occasions, having concern for his welfare.

As much as he wanted to protect his wife, he knew he couldn't. He felt helpless knowing that she would suffer.

His life had furnished him with endless positive experiences; although he didn't think they were at the time. He'd overcome many periods of adversity and learnt the purpose of sadness and despair. His torment had been contributory to his spiritual growth.

In essence, his abject loneliness and loss had led him to a unique moving forward in his life, where he'd experienced love on a higher level and found true happiness.

Reflecting on the times he'd confidently embraced his own individuality, he smiled. As a young teenager, his nonconformity had not been conducive with societal expectations.

Serge had an inexplicable feeling that this could be his final reincarnation. His connectedness with all the people in his life had been enriching.

Even his personal connection with periods of self-imprisonment, where his mental health had been tested to its limits, had brought about meaningful healing.

He'd felt that he'd experienced a totality; one

which had allowed his soul to progress into higher awareness.

His philosophical ponderings were abruptly interrupted by Hugo's arrival. Putting down his tools, he removed his mask.

"Bonjour Père. I see you've nearly finished it. I can't wait to see Suzette's face when you show it to her."

He nodded.

"You look exhausted. Have you finished for the day? It's time you rested."

He was tired. There'd be plenty of time to rest after he'd taken his last breath. He hoped he'd be able to last a while longer than the consultant had predicted.

He covered the nearly-finished creation with a dust sheet. He'd complete the finishing touches tomorrow and then he'd place removable cushions in the centre, so that it'd be comfortable for her when she sat on it.

Hugo linked his père's arm as they strolled back towards the kitchen terrace, where Nico and Suzette were waiting for them. His sorrow, at the inevitable loss, was as profound as when his maman had died. He couldn't bear the thought of losing him too.

Bravely, Serge spoke his thoughts.

"Your life doesn't need to be empty without me, son."

"But it will, Père. Much more than I care to imagine!"

"Use what I've taught you to guide your son throughout his life. Teach him the skills that my own father taught me. He has a great artistic flair, as you do. Help all those people who need you and fight their cause."

Hugo inhaled a deep breath, held it for a few seconds and exhaled. He'd rather not think about the future. Time was running out!

CHAPTER THIRTY SIX
May

They sat in relative silence, on the kitchen terrace, using hand gestures to communicate.

The mask relieved his chest pain and helped with his breathing.

Although Nico was curious to learn as much as he could about how the oxygen mask worked, he refrained from asking too many questions.

Somehow, Serge's pain seemed to diminish when his grandson was around. Seeing things from his perspective, made him feel stronger about the impending eventuality his family would have to deal with.

He'd no sooner removed the mask and unplugged the machine, when Nico initiated the conversation.

He'd been eavesdropping on his parent's conversations and wanted some answers.

"Grand-père, What will Grand-mère do when you die?"

Wanting to choose his words carefully, he paused before answering. They'd discussed death on previous occasions and he was acquainted with Nico's intelligent approach to the subject.

"She will be sad, but she'll be ok. She is a strong woman."

"Strong. Do you mean she can lift heavy things? Why would she need to do that?"

His unintentional lapse of disregarding Nico's literalness, had caused some confusion.

"What I meant to say was, that she will be ok, because you will all make sure that she is."

The little boy tendered another question.

"Are you frightened to die, Grand-père?"

This time, he carefully considered before answering.

"No. I'm not frightened. We all have to die sometime."

"I am so glad that you are not frightened. What will it be like? Do you think it will hurt you?"

Fascinated by Nico's questions, he curbed a smile.

"I don't know what it will be like, but I don't think it will hurt."

"That it good. I do not want it to hurt you."

His grandson's concerns played havoc with his emotions and he struggled to breathe.

"When you die, I will sing for you at your funeral."

This time, his tears escaped. As he reached for his handkerchief on the pretence of wiping his nose, he uttered his thanks.

"Oh! I thought I was going to sneeze then. Thank you, Nico."

Whilst trying to think of something to divert the conversation, he was thankful for his wife's appearance on the terrace. She'd been preparing lunch and, on hearing a little of the conversation which had filtered through the open window, had sensed Serge's need to be rescued.

"Are you ready to eat? Would you like to come and help me, Nico?"

Emotionally drained, he reached for his oxygen mask and placed it over his nose and mouth. The conversation had been heartbreaking, but it was necessary that the questions had been answered honestly.

He hadn't lied to his grandson. He wasn't frightened of dying; only disturbed by the sad thoughts of his wife's suffering after he'd died.

Having already discussed his expectations, he had requested that he should die at home. They'd spoken about his funeral and he'd decided on his choice of music. Cremation would take place and he'd prefer it if some of his ashes were made into personal pieces of jewellery for his family. They'd be free to create their own pieces. It was his way of remaining close to them all. He also wanted some of his ashes to be buried within the clearing under Oscillate; the moving sculpture his wife had created as a wedding gift for him. The remainder would be buried in the centre of the labyrinth beneath the triangular waterfall.

He quickly removed his mask. From where he was sat, he could see them returning and he didn't want them to witness him struggling to breathe.

CHAPTER THIRTY SEVEN
July

He'd received a spiritual communication earlier in the day, when he was ruminating at the labyrinth. Later that evening, he taken the opportunity to speak candidly with his wife as they snuggled on the sofa together.

"I'm aware that we reincarnate to earth school many times to learn from others; who are also there to accelerate our spiritual growth. I know it's a way of healing ourselves and helping others to heal too and that each of us have our own lessons to learn."

Allowing him to continue, she wondered where the conversation was leading.

"In many lives, I believe that some of us will keep on repeating the same harmful patterns of not learning. I've repeated those same patterns; I know I have. I realised it more when I completed your course with Gabriel and Eve."

"Why are you saying these things, Serge?"

He pondered for a few moments.

"Today, during meditation, I self-regressed to several lifetimes when we knew each other. Then, whilst I'm certain that I did love you, I rejected you many times. I'm so very sorry for what I did!"

Raising her eyebrows, she pursed her lips.

"My lack of emotional commitment must have been painful for you. No, it *was* painful for you. I could see it and yet I still rejected you!"

Unable to speak, she smiled at him.

"I even rejected you in this lifetime, when I first saw you walking along the Canal du Midi. Francesca had recently died and I was distraught – and quite drunk! Every other time you greeted me and waved, I didn't even acknowledge you. You must have thought I was impolite."

His frank confession penetrated her heart. She could hardly breathe. How could this adorable man have previously rejected her, when he adored her now? How had he found the courage to admit his weaknesses? She stared into his regretful eyes and saw the love and kindness in his soul, before answering him.

"I'm aware that when we reincarnate, we are given countless opportunities to exercise our own free will. Sometimes circumstances control our choices. What transpires then, is up to us," she whispered, as the frail butterflies quivered within her stomach.

Bracing herself, she sighed deeply, fearful of what else he might say.

"The time we've had together has been so very precious. You've enhanced my life in so many ways."

As she soaked up his every word, her pain was unbearable. Unable to stifle her sorrow, her screwed-up face exposed her utter torment, as her agony escaped from the corners of her eyes and flowed, uncontrollably, down her cheeks.

"The most important lesson that I've learnt this time was never to reject you again. I've also learnt not to repress my feelings. It destroyed me in my other lives. It destroyed all of our former relationships, when I callously abandoned you. I'm truly sorry. Forgive me."

She gazed at the man she loved. There was absolutely nothing to forgive. His apologies were unnecessary.

"I'm getting weaker, ma chérie. I'm not able to control this thing. It's controlling me. Whilst I'm doing my utmost to fight it, there are some days when I feel strong and, on other days, I'm so weak that I can't even think straight. Let's go to bed, Suzette. I'm tired."

Observing his escalating feebleness, she inhaled deeply and stiffened; trying to infuse some strength into her own weak body. She knew he was becoming more frail. Sometimes, he didn't have the energy to climb the stairs, but his willpower never let him falter and, this time was no different.

As was usual, he ascended the stairs to sleep with his wife in their marital bed.

Taking hold of her hand, he allowed her to assist him upstairs and to undress.

In silence, they lay side by side, in familiar embrace.

He was experiencing strange feelings.

"It's so surreal. I feel as if I'm floating. At times, I imagine my spirit leaving my body. My mind becomes blurred. I'm aware of people and sounds around me. I'm aware that you're with me, but I'm in a different place; a peaceful place."

"Stay with me for just a while longer, Serge. Please don't leave me yet", she pleaded.

"I'll do my best, ma chérie. I'll do my best. Let's sleep now."

Within a few moments he had drifted off.

Sleep evaded her. How could she sleep, when her brain felt as if it was expanding and trying to break through her skull? How could she sleep, if it was his time to leave her?

Her distressed heart pounded rapidly. She wanted to scream. She wanted her husband to live. How could she live without her man?

Moaning, she clung tightly onto him, before surrendering into the restless slumber that was beckoning her. Earnestly, she prayed that her cherished husband would live a little longer.

CHAPTER THIRTY EIGHT
July

He awoke before she did and watched her as she slept. He knew she needed her sleep. She couldn't sustain staying awake and watching over him all of the time. He knew she was shattered; in her mind as well as her body. The wrinkled shadows around her eyes and her furrowed brow did not belie her beauty. She was so very beautiful; on the inside and on the outside. Her selfless devotion to him and their family was expressed in everything she did.

He was satisfied that he'd fulfilled his pre-birth promise to her.

She opened her eyes; grateful that he was still there. As he smiled at her, she gasped.

"Thank you, God. You answered my pleas", she

whispered.

He'd heard what she'd said.

"Yes. Thank you, God. I'm glad my wife has had some sleep. It's strange, Suzette, but I feel a lot stronger this morning."

Quite the opposite to his extreme fatigue the evening before, his unexpected burst of energy was deceptively inexplicable.

Unaided, he moved to the edge of the bed and unsteadily walked to the bathroom.

On his return, he slipped his arms through his dressing robe and tentatively went downstairs.

Finding it hard to believe what she had just witnessed, she followed him, half expecting him to fall.

Trying hard not to excessively fuss over him, she watched as he poured boiling water over some peppermint leaves and allowed them to infuse.

"I think I'll try some bread and cheese for breakfast. Maybe a little apricot confiture too."

A feeling of wonderment engulfed her, as he prepared breakfast. His actions were bizarre.

"I think we should invite our family for an early afternoon tea?"

"Are you sure, Serge? Will you be ok?"

"Yes. I have much more energy today."

Feeling confused with the sudden change in him, she immediately rang Hugo and Eve and extended his invitation.

On hearing Suzette's voice, both of them had expected to hear the inevitable. Eagerly, they accepted.

At 3pm, a group of seven sat around the large dining table. Serge, albeit a frailer version of his former self, sat at the head of the table. Hugo, Sarah and Nico sat on one side and Eve and Gabriel sat opposite them. Suzette faced her husband, at the opposite end.

Just seeing them all sat around the table, induced flashbacks of the many happy times they'd celebrated together.

Surprisingly, the conversation flowed easily, as they spoke about what was happening in their lives.

Before raising his half-filled glass of Limoux, he managed to nibble at a lemon macaron.

"I'd like to thank you all for touching my life. You've all featured in some of the chapters in my life. I love each and every one of you."

He took a sip from his wine glass and could see that emotions were running high.

"Don't cry. I'm enjoying my last supper", he joked.

Nico approached Serge and tried to sit on his knee.

"Grand-père, shall we perform one of our favourite duets?"

"Yes, of course. I think we could do that."

With help from Hugo, he followed Nico over to the piano. Whilst the others watched in awe, the two of them played in harmony.

Noticing that her husband was weakening, she

walked over to the piano.

"I think Grand-père is a little tired now, darling."

Guiding Serge towards the sofa, she helped him to sit down.

Nodding to the others, they picked up on her message. It was time for them to leave.

Sensing that this would be the last time they saw him alive, they all said their goodbyes.

As they were leaving, Serge called out.

"I've had a wonderful afternoon. Thank you all for sharing it with me."

Hugo had some trouble persuading Nico to leave. He wanted to stay and was on the verge of having a serious meltdown.

Later that evening, as they snuggled on the sofa, she wondered if her husband would make it through the night.

"Let's go to bed, ma chérie. I'm exhausted."

Like on the previous nights, she supported his frail body as he struggled to climb the stairs.

On reaching their bedroom, he held tightly onto her and slowly shuffled her around the room.

"Our last dance, Suzette."

Trying to hide her sadness, she smiled as she undressed him and helped him into bed.

In the silence of the room, they lay in each other's arms until he fell asleep.

Sleep deprived as she was, she continued to watch over him until her weary body succumbed to a spiritually-tormented sleep.

CHAPTER THIRTY NINE
July

"Serge. Serge."

Inhaling a lengthy silence, she waited for a reply. None was forthcoming. She was mindful that her man was losing his fight for life.

"Don't leave me, darling. Not yet".

He tilted his head towards her and gradually opened his and closed his eyes.

"I'll hang on for as long as I can."

His once-strong, muscly frame was scrawny and almost lifeless as he lay, propped up on several pillows, in their marital bed.

Drowning in the depths of her impending grief, she began to question him, subconsciously.

"How much longer will I be able to look at your handsome face? How much longer will I be able to lie by your side and hold you?"

He reached out his hand for hers and his grip was weak. She lay closer to him, knowing that the end was imminent. Her brain was throbbing inside her skull, as she struggled to accept what was happening. How would she live without him? She didn't want to live without him.

"Lie closer, ma chérie."

Snuggling even closer, she laid her head on his bony shoulder, feeling every movement of his shallow breathing.

He spoke gently and slowly, continuing the conversation that they'd had two days earlier.

"Suzette. You know this is what we planned, before we reincarnated. We both agreed that I'd be the one to go first".

She gasped. She couldn't recollect any such conversation; but then she knew that her memory would've been wiped clean before her re-birth. Wrapping her arm across his chest, she could feel his ribcage underneath the drooping skin of his once-taut torso.

She wiped her eyes on the bed sheet.

"I don't remember, Serge. How could I ever have agreed to this? I'd gladly swap places with you now."

She leant over and kissed his lips gently and he responded by licking the flowing, salty tears from her face.

Subconsciously, he discerned that one of his soul's purposes was to advocate for people who were ill or had disabilities. By doing so, he knew that it would allow him to re-experience the imbalanced, emotional anguish which he had endured in his earlier lives and, in this one too!

Suzette had helped him to work through the traumatic challenges he'd been faced with and assisted him in overcoming them.

In meditation and in his sleeping dreams, he'd had several flashes of his existence in different human forms.

In those lives, he'd been rejected by people he loved. He thought they'd loved him too! He'd felt flawed and lacked self-respect. He'd also felt unimportant. A sensitive and vulnerable being, he'd been scared and powerless.

He knew that he'd reincarnated to conquer those feelings and to experience self-love.

"Ma chérie, I want you to know that being with you has allowed me to open my heart. I've learnt more about giving and receiving love. In my previous lives, I chose to tread a low-vibration path where love was definitely lacking. In this life, I've allowed myself to feel love and to give it too!"

She listened intently as he declared his own philosophy.

"At times it was extremely painful for me to love, especially when I repeatedly lost those who I'd loved; not forgetting those souls who were miscarried before even being born. It was equally as painful for Francesca. When you and I finally came together again, I allowed myself to genuinely embrace the feelings of being in love once more."

Whilst pausing for a few moments to catch his breath, he recalled how she'd first entered his life when he was at his lowest ebb and how she'd supported him in changing the way he processed his thoughts.

"You helped to me to recover from my mental health problems. I can accept now that all my difficulties weren't that meaningless."

He stopped again to catch his breath, before continuing.

"I've truly LIVED with you, ma chérie. I've appreciated every single moment we've shared."

His life was slowly ebbing away. Thankfully, the devastating disease hadn't yet reached his brain. Not wanting his family to witness his lucidity fade, he'd prayed that he'd die before it did!

The room smelled of him. It also smelled of frankincense and myrrh and impending finality.

Most of all, the air was juxtaposed with an intense feeling of love and sorrow; the latter being a grim emotion for Suzette to bear.

Her own breathing fell in keeping with his; trying with all her might to breathe some life into his limp body. She sensed, lying next to him, that this would be the last time that their hearts would beat together. Fatigued and lightheaded, her eyes closed and her weary body succumbed to slumber.

His soft whispering in her ear woke her. His body was cool, yet clammy. She noticed that his aura was different. Over the past few months, his aura had been lustreless. Now, she could see a wide, brilliant ethereal glow around him. It was twinkling and flashing randomly.

"Suzette. It's my time."

Within her heart, she knew what she was trying to do was wrong. Encouraging him to hold onto his life, for her sake, was inconsiderate when it was his time to go.

"Don't leave me, Serge. I want to come with you."

He struggled to speak.

"I've learnt all of what I've come on earth to learn. There's still so much work for you to do. You need to fulfil your agreement, before you can join me. There are others you have to reach; others who need you. Nico is just one of your priorities. Nurture him and help his soul to follow its path. Teach him what he needs to know to survive. He'll teach you many things too. The children in the school need you. Your family needs you."

She kissed his cold lips, which had turned blue.

"But *I need you*. Stay with me just a little longer", she begged selfishly.

His voice was fading.

"You know we'll see each other again. I've fulfilled my promise to you, ma chérie. I'll always be with you."

A heavy silence surrounded her as she clung to him distraughtly, not wanting him to leave her. His gentle voice resounded in her ears. She was frightened. She'd never hear him pronounce her name the way he did in his distinct, dulcet tone.

Intuitively, she focused all her energy and her love onto him to assist him on his return to spirit. As she did so, the familiar, pulsating sound in her ears reverberated around her head and her whole body tingled.

She continued to lie closely against his still-warm body, with her hand over his chest, until she could no longer feel him breathing.

It was a surreal moment. She could see his spirit leaving his body, floating into the ether. A white, opaque figure was also accompanying on his journey 'back home'.

In the abject coldness of the bedroom, she trembled as she reached for the telephone.

Shivering with shock, her incoherent words strangled her as Gilbert answered.

"Serge has gone. Can you come over?"

"Yes. I'll come now."

Next, she rang Hugo and Eve.

Outside, the blazing Mediterranean sun was beating down on their garden, the cicadas were chirping in the trees and the plants and flowers still thrived; all unaware of Serge's passing. Nothing would ever be the same for her. Yes, life would go on for her and for many others, but she also knew that her husband's absence would be greatly felt by those who loved him.

Absent-mindedly, she pressed the red 'off' button on her phone.

She could hear his voice.

"I'm still here. I'm still with you."

Within her woeful heart, she knew he'd always be with her in spirit.

Returning to his lifeless form, she lay down at the side of him and held his body for the last time.

CHAPTER FORTY
July

His voice echoed in her ears and it found a place in every crevice of their bedroom. His smell and his presence lived on in every room, in every flower and plant, in his atelier and in their own sacred sanctuary within the clearing.

She knew his visits would be a comfort to her through the coming days, months and years!

On lonely nights, before his funeral, she creatively re-lived her precious memories in an imaginary film, which she played over and over again until she fell asleep.

This evening was different. She'd tossed and turned; first sleeping on her own side of the bed and then moving onto the side where Serge had slept. She ached for him.

A buzzing noise vibrated within her ears and a tingle travelled down the length of her spine. A clear orb had entered the room and was moving towards her. She sensed it was him. Even in spirit, there was a chemistry which made her heart sing and her hormones dance. It was as if he knew that she needed him.

"Is that you, Serge?"

His soothing voice reassured her as the orb transformed into an ethereal form and came to stand at the side of her bed.

"Yes, ma chérie."

She closed her eyes tightly. On opening them again, he was still there.

"Lie by my side. Hold me"

As she moved over from his side of the bed, she felt his presence, as a warm feeling enveloped her and his arms encompassed her weary body. She felt his face against her cheek, soothing her. She could feel his hand lightly tilting her chin and as his lips gently touched hers, she felt calm and safe.

"I *am* holding you, Suzette. Try to sleep."

His timely visit and his infusion of energy had provided her with some temporary comfort. The fatigue which had kept her company for the last few days, whilst she prepared for his funeral, slowly dissipated.

In the spiritual arms of her newly-deceased husband, her own spirit was transcended into a place of deep slumber; protecting her for the time being from her unwelcome situation.

The following morning, the small carving which he'd sculpted for her was positioned on the pillow at the side of her.

Last evening, it had been on the bedside table.

Her heart flipped. She picked it up and held it close to her chest.

He'd given her another sign that he hadn't left her!

CHAPTER FORTY ONE
July

The following night, she dreamed of him again. He'd told her to look in his personal drawer.

Stepping out of bed, she walked over to the old chest of drawers that contained his personal papers.

On opening the top drawer, she saw two envelopes resting on top of several handkerchiefs.

Picking them up, she brought them to her nostrils. They smelled of him.

Slowly, she ran her fingers across her name on each of them. He'd never write her love letters again! She let out a heavy sigh, as an emptiness engulfed her chest and a buzzing noise throbbed within her ears.

She didn't have the emotional strength to read

them yet. Her mental state wouldn't allow her to read whatever he'd written. She'd leave them until later.

Placing the treasured envelopes under her pillow, she went into the bathroom to rinse her face.

As she entered the kitchen, her expectance of him being there, singing as he was preparing breakfast, made her feel resentful. Engulfed in her grief, a stabbing sensation pierced her stomach as she frantically scanned the room, willing him to be there. She wrapped her arms around her stomach and bent over to try and ease the pain.

Sarah had wanted to stay with her until after the funeral, but she needed to be alone with her grief. She didn't have the strength to talk, other than to make the necessary arrangements for his cremation.

She even wondered where she'd find the strength to get through his funeral. She'd have to remain strong and eat something, if she was going to carry her husband's coffin with Hugo, her son, and her son-in-law. It was the last thing she could do for him!

She switched the radio on. Someone was singing La Vie En Rose. On their wedding the day, the band had played the exact song for their first dance together as a married couple. Serge was sending her another sign.

Walking into the pantry, she picked up some walnut bread, which Sarah had brought for her the previous evening.

Absentmindedly, whilst slicing through the bread, she managed to cut through the tip of her middle finger on her right hand.

Quickly, she grabbed a wad of kitchen roll, to stem the blood that was streaming from the cut.

After cleansing the wound and dressing it with a plaster, she took the bread and a chunk of cheese from the fridge and sat at the table.

She couldn't face eating. The bread choked her as she swallowed it, but she forced it down, continuing to eat until the plate was empty.

"Come on, Suzette. You can do this. You can", she encouraged herself.

She opened the kitchen door and stepped outside into the morning sun. The warmth seemed to soothe her a little and she strolled over to the garden seat that he'd sculpted for her.

The strength she'd had whilst she'd nursed him, seemed to have left her. Fragility wasn't part of her persona; but her arms felt noticeably weak and a numbness had planted itself inside her legs, making it difficult for her to walk steadily.

Aiming to regain her balance, she sat down and tried to make sense of the emotional turmoil that had impacted her happiness.

Closing her eyes, she inhaled and exhaled several deep breaths, before entering a profound meditative state.

Somewhere in the elongated corridors of her subconscious, she recollected the promise. It was both intriguing and illogical.

In spirit, before reincarnating, they were sat together at a table discussing how things would transpire when they met up again in human form.

There was another spirit standing behind them, smiling and offering them guidance and support.

His voice reinforced what they'd just agreed.

"This is just one part of the many paths you will tread. You'll experience many challenges."

In spirit, she'd offered to be the one who would be left behind when the other one died.

This particular suffering and heartbreak would be another part of her spiritual growth.

Her mind wandered, reflecting on how much she'd already endured whilst she'd been travelling along her path in this lifetime. Likewise, she had embraced many joyful events, whilst experiencing different kinds of love.

Re-experiencing the pre-birth meeting with Serge was extraordinary.

They'd talked about their journeys and the time and the place where they'd meet up again.

They would eventually discover the genuine depth and strength of their love this time. Her meditative state was interrupted when she heard Nico's voice.

"Grand-mère. I am here now. I told you I would come. I have just been out walking with my père. He gave me permission to come to see you. What shall we do today?"

He sat at the side of her and leant into her chest, transferring his strength into the bones of her grief-torn body.

Intuitively, she knew that this little boy would be the motivation for her to get up each day and stay alive.

"I'm hungry, Grand-mère."

"Are you, darling. Haven't you eaten your breakfast?"

"Yes, but I'm still hungry."

She spoke softly to her grandchild.

"Well, Nico. Let's go inside and find you something to eat."

In his own mind, he knew exactly what he was doing. He wanted to make sure that she was eating, even if he had to uncomfortably forego his rigid routine and eat again; so soon after having his breakfast. When he'd cuddled her, he'd noticed that she was very thin!

"Do you think we could bake some of our favourite madeleines, Grand-mère?"

As they meandered back towards the house, he slipped his hand into hers and guided her along the meditation path. Her heart did a double back-flip and, as she looked into his soulful brown eyes, his look of innocence gave her some hope.

****

Lying on their marital bed that evening, she tentatively reached under the pillow for one of the envelopes. Just knowing that his hands had touched it and the way he'd written her name in bold letters on the front, made her shiver as she opened it. Unfolding the two perfectly pleated sheets of parchment paper, she'd only managed to read the first few paragraphs before her vision became blurred.

Ma chérie,

Je t'aimerai pour toujours. I know you will be missing me, but always remember, I treasured every single moment we shared. The strong connection we had is unbreakable. It can never be severed.

Her hands trembled as she carefully folded the sheets of paper and placed them back inside the envelope. She wasn't strong enough to read the rest of what he'd written; not yet!

Curious as to what was contained in the other envelope, she opened it. Inside, were instructions as to where he'd left some personal possessions.

She opened the top drawer of his cabinet and she rummaged under a neat pile of carefully folded, sweaters. Nestled between two sheets of paper, was a line drawing of her lying under the lemon trees in Italy.

Grasping it to her chest, she ached for him.

The unannounced flashback was unbearable.

She bent over and rocked backwards and forwards, as the gnawing emptiness ripped into her guts.

CHAPTER FORTY TWO
14 July

After a sleepless night, she rose early and went straight to the labyrinth. Today was going to be a tough one to get through.

Sitting there amongst his creations, craving his presence, she reflected on her life with him.

The morning sun still forced its way through the gaps in the trees, but the sun had gone out of her life. The birds still chirped and fluttered their wings as they flew above her, but she'd never feel his unforeseen, fluttering kisses on her lips, on her cheeks, on the tip of her nose, the nape of her neck and her breasts as he teased her; except perhaps, when he came to visit her in spirit.

Her inner voice spoke to her.

"Try to be strong. You can do this."

Within her subconscious, memories of her life with him flew past her, like a reel-to-reel of old film being jerkily projected onto a cinema screen; not too dissimilar to the way her uncontrollable heartbreak had jerked intermittently through the entirety of her body, since he'd died.

Her eyes scanned the whole of the clearing. Everything in this space had been lovingly created by him; especially for her! It was still the same. Absolutely nothing had changed. Yet, absolutely everything had changed!

Walking over to the summer house, she stepped inside. Feeling numb and vulnerable, she wondered how she'd cope without him.

Even though it was a warm morning, she shivered uncontrollably. Taking a fluffy blanket out of the storage box, she wrapped it tightly around her shoulders and rocked back and forth in slow motion; in an effort to temporarily soothe her gnawing grief.

She had an urge to scream loudly, but she didn't have the energy to expel the intense pain that was embedded in the pit of her stomach.

She looked down at her watch. It was time nearly time.

Forcing herself to leave her sacred space, she walked slowly back to the house, to face the overwhelming, imminent event of her husband's funeral.

In times of loss, she'd built a wall around herself; a wall which was as high as it was wide.

She could feel that same wall closing in around her again. She knew her family were concerned about her. She could feel their pain. She had to let them in; she had to. She'd try. They missed him too!

****

Following a sun-filled morning, the rain had started to fall around 11:00am and had continued to drizzle as the black hearse, carrying her cherished husband's coffin, manoeuvred slowly through the entrance gates of the crematorium.

She shivered as she stepped out of the car. The soulful sound of Nico playing the organ filtered through the open doors. As his final gift to his Grand-père, he would sing and perform his own rendition of 'The Prayer', as well as some of the music which they'd composed together.

With her inner voice encouraging her to retain her feigned dignity, she took several deep breaths. Purposely adorning an imaginary mask, with the solitary intention of camouflaging her psychological vulnerability, she tried to conceal the fact that, inside, she was finding it extremely hard to cope!

Several, irrepressible shudders moved through her fatigued body. She forced herself to stand upright, in readiness to accept her husband's body from the four subdued-looking undertakers, as they slid his coffin from the rear of the hearse.

Taking her place at the front, she gripped the handles on his coffin and turned to see Yoshio behind her. She'd always had a strong connection with her son-in-law. On the opposite side, she witnessed the pain on Hugo and Alex's tear-stained faces, as they also gripped tightly onto the handles.

Struggling to contain her tears, she moved forward. The impact of her recent loss threatened to violently erupt, as she carefully carried his body through the double doors.

Nico's fingers rested on the keys until the right moment. His angelic voice welcomed them as he started to sing.

"Grand-père, I'll pray you'll be alright."

Her trembling hands gripped the handles, as her inner voice encouraged her to remain strong.

She focused on the funeral director as he slowly guided them towards a heavy, steel-framed, moveable platform which was positioned in the centre of the chapel.

The room started to spin as she lowered the coffin. Lightheaded and weak, she managed to locate a chair and sat down. She didn't want to make a scene. Nevertheless, she wasn't in control of how her mind and body were reacting to losing Serge.

The words of the song resonated with the way she felt.

"When shadows fill our day."

She knew she should have eaten something before she left, but the thought of putting food into her mouth only increased the already existing nausea that had become her constant companion.

Unable to envisage her life without him, again

she inhaled deeply before letting out a long, loud sigh.

From out of nowhere, a soothing calmness surrounded her. It was as if a cloak of numbness was being wrapped tightly around the whole of her body; protecting her.

The tempo of the music slowed, as he sang the last line.

"Give us faith, so we'll be safe."

The droning mumblings of the minister's voice reverberated inside the chapel, as he rigidly followed the script which he held in front of him.

She was brought abruptly to her senses as she heard him introduce Hugo and Nico.

As she listened to them both reading their carefully written eulogies, her son's already-draped arm around her shoulder, tightened. He held onto her hand, whilst her daughter leant in close and lovingly linked her arm through hers.

It didn't seem that long ago that Hugo had read his mother's eulogy in the very same chapel.

In turn, Guy, Gaston, Thierry and Gabriel also expressed their love for Serge; relaying fond memories of their younger years, when his natural ability to play tricks and make them laugh would sometimes get them into trouble.

In the midst of it all, she intuitively sensed him hovering over them; watching his own funeral.

Bizarrely, the platform slowly started to roll backwards. Hugo leapt out of his seat to stop it.

Having earlier witnessed it being secured, they

looked around at each other and smiled. He'd sent them a communication; his final humorous output.

As the minister brought the ceremony to a conclusion, she arose from her seat and stood by her husband's coffin. Resting her hand on it, she managed to stem her tears as Nico skillfully began to play, 'The Long and Winding Road'. Serge had sung that very same song to her on her wedding day. He was forever singing the words or humming the tune.

Gabriel started singing and they all followed suit; patting the coffin in fond farewell as they walked past Suzette.

Insightfully, today, she related to last line of the song to the ending of his human life. He was being led towards the door which would take him back to his spiritual home.

Wanting a final moment with her husband, she lingered. Bending down, she kissed his coffin and, this time, she allowed her tears to flow.

Nico finished playing and walked towards her.

Taking her handkerchief from inside her bag, she wiped her eyes. Holding hands, they both walked away, without looking back.

Outside, the sun was shining, the drizzle had cleared and an arching, ethereal rainbow was visible in the sky. Taking it as a spiritual sign for his re-birth, she acknowledged his message.

Standing apart from the rest of them for a few moments, she watched as Nico ran over to Hugo. In going through her own vulnerability and pain, she suddenly experienced a compassionate vibration for their family and friends, who were also grieving.

As if sensing that any show of their own emotions would intensify hers, they allowed her some time alone to compose herself.

Having received messages of condolence, commending his exceptional, creative talent and his geniality, she imagined those people in the art world would also mourn his passing.

Yes, he'd be missed by many and yet she knew that his life would always be connected to everyone who'd known him and those people who had met him.

CHAPTER FORTY THREE
July

At Serge's request, the reading of his will had taken place five days after his funeral.

His ashes had been placed in a wooden urn in the centre of the table.

Following a brief introduction, the notary had informed those present that, whilst the estate and his belongings automatically passed on to Suzette, he'd bequeathed some personal items and monetary sums to his family and friends.

Hugo would inherit his car, an open-topped blue Citroën Traction Avant. The car had been gifted to Serge when his uncle had died and it hadn't been used that much; except for short drives to the coast and on his wedding day when he drove Suzette into Lezignan to take their vows.

It had been carefully stored in the garage, covered with a large dust sheet and polished occasionally.

Serge's larger sculptures would remain in the museum in Collioure, alongside other famous artists' creations.

The smaller pieces had been collected and were safely stored in his atelier, ready for his close friends and family to choose from.

The tools of his trade had been left to Nico and Hugo with a request that they follow in his footsteps. Also, he'd donated a substantial amount of money, for research into how creative projects would benefit the development of children with autism and learning differences. Sessions could be delivered in his atelier.

Personal items and equal monetary sums had been left to all members of his family.

A monetary donation was allocated to the hospital in India, where Eve and Gabriel had volunteered their services.

As discussed previously, some of his ashes would be taken to a designer in Narbonne, who'd agreed to incorporate them into pieces of jewellery as mementos for his family.

The rest of his ashes would be buried in and around his beloved labyrinth.

After the notary had left, they ate a light lunch and chatted late into the afternoon about Serge's life.

With her family and friends around her, she felt less vulnerable, but she knew once her children and grandchildren had returned to their homes, that her intense grieving would leave her fragile.

Whilst her family were sleeping, she crept outside and went inside his atelier. Sitting there with his tools scattered around, was comforting.

She flicked through some charcoal drawings which were in a pile on the end of his workbench. All seemed to relate to his impending death.

One particular sketch depicted his own lung cancer. Other illustrations were of fluffy clouds and ethereal beings.

The last one she picked up was one of himself, walking along a path.

She pressed the drawing close to her chest and sobbed uncontrollably. At the time of drawing, when they had been on holiday just before his diagnosis, he'd intuitively known his life's journey was coming to an end.

CHAPTER FORTY FOUR
August

She'd been pottering in the garden all morning and had sat down to rest on the bench that Serge had crafted for her. The physical activity of being with nature and tending to her plants was a distraction.

After his death, her emotional agitation had all but dominated her waking and sleeping moments. The intermittent fear of entering the unknown, of living without him, was manipulating her muddled mind and making her confused.

A sudden wave of realisation swept over her and she felt as if she was drowning. No one could save her; only herself!

Sitting for a while with her grief, instead of shutting it out, she somehow managed to confront the situation. She allowed her situation to present her with more lessons; although it was enormously challenging to retain a balance between surviving and sinking.

Recollecting her younger-life experiences, she compared them with the life she was living at the moment. Putting everything into perspective, she knew that every minute, every second was relevant.

Smiling, she recalled a former telephone call from her friend in Ireland

"Serge isn't real. He's too perfect. There's not a man on this earth who is like him!"

He'd been real enough to her. Yes, they'd had their differences of opinions on several occasions, but they'd never held onto the irrelevant stuff. In fact, those trivial disparities that had occasionally occurred, had only brought subtle shifts into their relationship and they'd become more compatible.

From time to time, irritations would surface, but those irritations were part of what they'd loved about each other. They'd trusted each other, they'd discovered things about each other, they'd been attentive to each other's needs.

She sensed his presence.

"Bonjour darling".

"Bonjour, ma chérie. Don't be sad. I'm not in any pain. It's so peaceful here, Suzette."

She yearned to be with him.

"Just after I'd left you, I was still hovering around for a while. Then, two spirits came to greet me. They asked me what I'd learnt whilst I was on earth."

"What did you say?"

"I told them that I'd learnt to feel pain and endure the suffering that came with it. I'd learnt to accept life as it happened and to forgive. I'd learnt to give love and receive love. I told them that when I was with you, I'd found my true self. I'd also learnt to unlearn my negative resentment and any unreasonable expectations, of what, who and how I thought I should be. This place is full of profound love. I'm understanding now that love is one of the greatest lessons we all need to learn. Death is nothing to be afraid of."

Her awareness of eternal consciousness and spirit, was genuine enough for her to know that what he was saying was true. Yet, her human form had temporarily blocked out the capacity for her to learn from her recent loss and all she felt, was immense pain.

At this moment, her overwhelming need for him was far stronger than her existing belief that her hurting would heal in time.

With tears already misting her eyes, she released her pain and let it drift into the trees behind where she was sitting.

"I miss you, Serge. I *am* really trying hard to adjust to my life without you. I'm fully aware that dealing with it is one of my soul's lessons, but it's unbearable at times. I know my path isn't meant to be easy, but I wasn't prepared for this eventuality."

She sank deeper into the thickly-padded

cushions and hugged herself.

"Nico keeps me moving forward. When he's not at school, he's constantly at my side. His constant chattering about other lifetimes and other cultures are incredible."

"Suzette, I want you to know something. Nico was your son in previous lifetimes. You've shared many lives together. I've shared some of them with both of you. His decision to reincarnate, was to thank you for understanding him and allowing him to live his own life the last time you were together.

He's sorry for rejecting you time after time and he wished he hadn't hurt you with his reckless behaviour. He bitterly regrets not being with you in the last lifetime you shared, when you acquired a disability and died alone."

Receptive of the spiritual communication, she'd already sensed that there'd been shared history with her grandson as soon as he was born. The connection had been profound. The uncanny way he'd said things about them being together before and the random occasions that he'd called her Maman, had also alerted her to the possibility.

"In this lifetime, Nico has reincarnated to experience the challenges that disability brings; not a physical disability like the one you had, but a neurological difference."

In her self-regression, several days ago, two words have been given to her; REJECTION and ALONE.

The message she'd received then, was now

relevant. She sent up a silent thank you.

"You've got to know that my human death hasn't parted us, Suzette. I'm still with you."

Perhaps one of her lessons to learn was to accept rejection. Another lesson to learn was to embrace solitude. The latter had been effortless before her husband had died. It took more of an effort to enjoy her own company, since he'd gone.

His favourite song started to resound inside her head, as his spirit left her to contemplate his message.

Satori* had visited her once again. It had been a constant visitor over the past thirty years.

Observing the stark reality of her situation and identifying all the wonderful things she had in her life, she recognised that she'd been given another sign; nudging her to accept what had happened. There was no alternative. Moving forward was the only path she needed to tread.

Silently, she prayed.

"Please, God. Help me to endure this pain in my heart and give me the courage to carry on."

She had to allow the catalytic change to flow. It was inevitable.

She'd endeavour to put into practice what she preached.

*spiritual awakening

CHAPTER FORTY FIVE
August

The iridescent pebbles glistening in the stream and the cooling, marble path on her bare feet, were reminiscent of the very first time she'd stepped onto it.

Again, she'd wandered through the fruit trees and vegetable patches, imagining him being there; willing him to be there. The gentle breeze brushed against her face, as she meandered along the meditation path to their special place.

Sitting alone in the centre of the labyrinth, she tried to concentrate on being in the present; attempting to accept that there was no escape from what her life really was. Practising on a daily basis, was a norm for her. She followed her own approach to living. Searching within, was her spiritual custom of understanding her true self. Incorporating meditation with her own spiritual beliefs, didn't necessarily slot her into any specific religion. Speaking with God, her spirit guides and other spirits who communicated with her, was a regular occurrence.

She meditated; not to clear her mind, but to focus her mind and become more aware. It wasn't easy when her mind persisted in revisiting recent events.

She picked up her pencils and sketchbook. Drawing several images, she coloured them in and made several notes alongside them.

As a Jungian disciple, she was aware of the significance of automatic writing and drawings; and the revealing effect they had on her healing and self-discovery. Dreams, songs, images and symbols also featured strongly in her approach to daily life.

Stopping for a moment, she listened to the sound of the water echoing, as it trickled down the sides of the sculpture. Leaning over, she allowed the cold drops to pass through her fingers.

Appreciating the silence, she sat quietly with her sadness. The tranquility didn't alter the reality that she was grieving deeply, but it did help her to face the days ahead.

She'd had a few good days where she felt she could cope and then some days, like today, her grief overwhelmed her.

Her head was throbbing. Placing her arms around her slumped shoulders, she hugged herself.

She didn't want to think. She didn't want to eat. She didn't want to live – without him.

Never had she imagined that loss could be so destructive.

Even though she understood that human suffering was part of life, the magnitude of her loss had tightly gripped her mind and seized her body; crushing her, smothering her, destroying her!

Confronting her pain, she sobbed again. She didn't judge herself for allowing the many facets of her human fallibility to surface.

Her inner voice encouraged her.

"Come on, Suzette. He hasn't abandoned you. It was his time to go. Don't allow yourself to become a victim. Change is inevitable for all of us."

She thought of one of Carl Gustav Jung's quotes, 'We cannot change anything, unless we accept it'.

Using self-hypnosis to diminish some of the pain, she imagined a healing light penetrating the top of her head and moving downwards towards her heart. Closing her eyes, she discerned that his death would be a lesson of acceptance.

Unaware of Nico's presence, she answered herself, "I'll try to accept. I'll try."

He'd clearly heard her mournful self-talk, before he'd caught sight of her hunched-up body.

Leaning over, he wrapped his arms around her shoulders and held her tightly. He kissed her face and her head.

Opening her eyes, she gazed at him.

"Grand-mère. I will take care of you."

Ever since Serge had died and, even before, he'd been incredibly protective of her.

She hadn't wanted him to see her like this. He was grieving too. He was the child and she was the adult. She should be comforting him.

Straightening her torso, she lifted him onto her knee. Drawing his small body into her chest, she rocked him gently. The dampness from the tears, which had fallen onto the top of her dress, pressed against his cheek and he wiped his face.

He looked up at her and studied her face.

"Grand-mère."

"Yes, darling."

"Did you know that you have lots of wrinkly lines around your eyes and your mouth?"

"Have I, Nico?"

"Yes. There are hundreds of lines on your forehead too!"

She chuckled. His ability to detect the finest of details was another of his traits and his honest use of words had lightened her spirit.

Not knowing what she was laughing at, he laughed with her. Taking hold of her hand, he gripped it tightly.

Following their humorous moment, they sat in silence, watching the oscillating triangles move back and forth in the moderate breeze.

She'd often wondered, when younger, why triangles had featured in almost every phase of her life. Considering that they signified change and creativity, they were relevant. Change had been a constant caller in her life. Change had motivated her to include the geometric shapes in the design of her kinetic sculpture.

In the weeks previous to Serge's passing, the triangles had moved frantically. The wind had blown furiously and they'd struggled to regain their balance. It was as if the moving, mobile structure had sensed the forthcoming, tragic event and was teaching her another lesson; that life is what it's supposed to be. It fluctuates.

She'd known then, that the winds of change would cause disruption in her life; although she hadn't envisaged the true extent. If she could just allow herself to surrender to the ebb and flow of human oscillation, maybe she'd feel that she was healing.

He leant over and whispered in her ear; his words echoing the ever-present thoughts of her own sorrowful yearning.

"I miss Grand-père, too."

The formality in his voice made him sound older. Yet he was still a little boy; a boy with an adult persona and an astuteness beyond his years.

Her grandson's kindness towards her and others was special. He wasn't aware of his aspiring humanity; although she'd witnessed it many, many times. He was so caring, especially with Xavier and Enzo.

He'd also sat with Serge and comforted him during his final weeks of life. They'd read poetry and played duets on the piano. He'd performed recitals and raised money for people less fortunate than himself.

As if he didn't have enough challenges to overcome; he'd put others before himself.

"Grand-mère, can I tell you something?"

"Yes, darling. What is it?"

"Grand-père came to me just after he died. I saw him and he hugged me. I already knew when Père told me about him later."

"Did he, darling?"

"Yes. Can I tell you something else?"

"Yes, please do."

"I have lived with you before; many times."

Smiling, she nodded her head.

"I have, honestly. I did. I did. In one lifetime, you were my maman. I was a little girl then and you taught me how to sew and design clothes. You encouraged me to work hard for what I believed in. In that lifetime, when I grew up, I created garments for royalty. We lived in Paris."

Unsurprised by his disclosure, she nodded.

"Do you believe me?"

"Of course, I do."

"In another lifetime, you were an artist. I was your son and you were my père. We were very poor and we did not have much money. We did not eat properly. You were so dedicated to your art, that we both died of cold and starvation in a cave in the mountains."

Raising her eyebrows, she inhaled several

times, before allowing him to continue. It would seem that her existing creative streak had featured in many of her past lives.

"When I was with you last time, I was your only son and, when my père died, we went to live in a small apartment. When your illness left you disabled and you couldn't care for yourself, I had to do most things for you. I was ten years old and I can remember pushing your heavy wheelchair. I was embarrassed to be seen pushing you around."

His honest portrayal overwhelmed her. She genuinely believed that Nico's collective, inborn memories and his psychic energy, were related to his high level of intelligence and creative skills.

"Some children would laugh at me. They would call us horrible names. I missed an awful lot of schooling and playing out with my best friend, but you taught me my lessons at home."

Nodding, she encouraged him to continue.

"When I got older, I left you to go travelling with my friend; having adventures. You gave me your blessing and I left you. I did not know how sad you would be without me. You had some people coming in to check on you, but you must have been extremely lonely. When you died an early death, you were on your own. I am very sorry."

She pulled him closer. Nico didn't attempt to conceal his advanced psychic abilities, even when he was with others.

"I have made some mistakes, Grand-mère. Please forgive me. I am truly sorry."

His doleful eyes exposed his repentance and she reassured him.

"We don't make mistakes, Nico. We have experiences, from which we learn. Nothing is a mistake. Life lessons happen every day. We learn from sad events and happy ones too, you know!"

He raised his thumbs and shook his hands.

"You don't have to keep saying sorry."

Shrugging his shoulders, he placed his hand over his mouth. Recently, he'd been attempting to conquer his repetitive acts of apologising, but he wasn't having much success.

"I will try not to, Grand-mère."

"Well, that's a sensible thing to do."

He listened intently as she described vivid scenes from her own childhood in this lifetime.

She was astounded when he joined in the conversation, illustratively painting a verbal picture of the locations she was talking about.

She was further startled, when he conveyed personal details about specific events which had occurred in her life; even providing exact names of those who'd been involved.

In absolute respect of his intuitiveness, she genuinely believed that Nico's clairvoyance ability was added confirmation, that he'd been blessed with the gift of living his life as a spiritual healer.

Taking hold of his hands, she noticed that his palms were hot and slightly swollen. Feeling his energy transferring into her own hands, a series of vibrations inside her ears also verified the strong spiritual connection they had

As they sat in silence, she deduced that he was, undeniably, an old soul. The way in which he enjoyed being around older people, continually questioning about various enigmatic events, was just one indication. His introverted practice of occupying his own time, his repetitive reading, his retention of knowledge and appreciation of history were other signs.

Acceptance of his connections to the past seemed natural for him and his concerned interest in human sciences, also drew attention to Suzette's assumption that 'he'd definitely been here before'.

"Did I tell you about how this wonderful place came about?"

Proceeding to relay the story of how Serge had thoughtfully re-structured the clearing and created the meditation path and labyrinth for her as a wedding present, she again described in great detail, how she'd specifically designed Oscillate as her wedding gift to him.

Nico had heard the story endless times.

On this occasion, he patiently listened to every word, without any interruptions; although his feet were uncontrollably tapping in tune, whilst he constantly fidgeted and arranged some twigs he'd found nearby.

As she began to recite her poem, which explained the meaning behind the moving mobile structure, he recited it with her. Although he didn't understand it, he'd memorised every single word.

To and fro
Back and forth
Ebb and flow

Human oscillation
Perpetual routines
Reluctance to shift

Unforeseen friction
Sanity provoked
Forcing imperative change

Indecisive, unsettled
Undulating, erratic
Resisting the flow

Impromptu awakening
Recognition takes place
Transition unfolds

Freedom is felt
Equilibrium intact
Oscillation restored

To and fro
Back and forth
Ebb and flow

"Shall I sing for you, Grand-mère? The one about the prayer?"

"Yes, I'd like that very much."

"Do you know that if you hold on tightly to your memories, they will give you some comfort."

She smiled at his grown-up advice and his needing to fix her hurting. She'd need to fix that herself!

"I'll do as you say. I'm sure they will."

Recalling the many times, she and Serge had been together in their sanctuary, she smiled. Her memories would, most definitely, keep her strong. She felt that she'd never get over losing him, but she'd live with him inside her heart. If she could accept that the upheaval was just another step on her journey, she might then be able to focus on allowing things to happen. With time, she felt that her anguish would gradually lessen. She'd work through it. She had no choice!

As the dappled sunlight filtered through the trees, she listened as he vocally warmed-up by humming the tune, before clearly articulating the words; praying that she'd be alright.

His angelic voice was another snippet of joy which would carry her safely along her path.

CHAPTER FORTY SIX
August

Ambling mindlessly amongst the bustling market stalls in Lezignan, she gazed over at the bar where she'd met him on that wonderous afternoon many years ago; the afternoon when the hands of fate had finally brought them back together and her life had taken on a new meaning.

She walked over and sat on the chair in the exact position where she'd sat that very day. Every single second of the encounter and the subsequent events of that day came flooding back. In her mind's eye, she recollected several vivid images and the emotional association of that meeting, catapulted her weakened nervous system into overdrive. They'd drank champagne and then he'd kindly invited her back to his home. Following a substantial meal, she'd impulsively propositioned him. Eagerly, they'd joined together on the rough grass under the early evening sunlight. She knew then that they'd be together.

The waiter came over to her. Ironically, it was the very same waiter who'd served her on that memorable afternoon. Franco was sympathetically mindful of her recent loss and he'd soon fathomed the reason for her usual visits to his café bar on Wednesdays.

"Bonjour, Madame. Ca va? Que voulez-vous boire?"

"Bonjour. Pas bon aujourd'hui, Franco."

She respected Franco's concern. Every time she frequented the café, he asked how she was feeling. Every time she responded with the same answer. She wasn't feeling good.

"Je vais avoir une petite bière s'il vous plait."

She ordered a small beer; the same as she'd ordered on the day she'd first spoken with Serge. In her own mind, she was recreating that occasion.

Franco returned with the beer and placed it in front of her. On most occasions, he'd initiate a conversation with her. At other times, he'd smile understandingly, leaving her to her thoughts. This was one of those times!

Subconsciously, she questioned herself.

"Why is it, that on some days I feel strong and on other days I feel so fearfully fragile?"

As he strode back into the bar, she pictured Serge sitting opposite her, smiling. She recalled the conversation and how his face had lit up when he'd discovered that they shared many similar interests.

She fondly remembered how she'd caught him snatching glances of her, when he thought she wasn't looking and the way her heart had missed a beat when he'd asked if he could come over and sit with her.

Clearly recollecting every single detail, she imagined his collar length, silver hair and the chic way in which he wore his black and white linen shirt with broad, distinctive stripes, tucked into his black chino shorts. The collar was open and it had revealed his hairy chest. She'd been aroused by his manliness and how he'd pronounced her name in his distinct French tone.

A sudden sob threatened to choke her as it attempted to escape from her throat. Her knees trembled as the dreaded angst decided to visit her once again. As she composed herself, intermittent ripples of insecurity left her feeling very uncertain of her future.

Tingling in her face and arms alerted her that something was about to happen; as did the unwanted palpitations in her heart and her rapid shallow breathing.

She knew that, if she didn't take control, the hyperventilation would take over and she'd faint; leaving her with an even more intense feeling of vulnerability.

It was imperative that she concentrated on controlling her breathing. She closed her eyes and, performing the same trusted technique she used in meditation, she inhaled numerous deep breaths, allowing the oxygen to fill her diaphragm, before exhaling again.

Managing her symptoms successfully, she regained control and, as she opened her eyes, she could see Franco coming towards her with a glass of water. He'd been watching her from inside.

"Suzette. Vous sentez-vous malade? Puis-je vous aider?"

Grateful for Franco's concern and his offer of help, she nodded and smiled.

"Merci Franco. Je vais bien maintenant. Juste un petit vertige."

Explaining to him that she'd felt a little dizzy, but the moment had passed, Franco sat with her for a while, holding her hand. He wanted to make sure that she was ok. On recent occasions, he'd experienced her untimely fainting episodes and was concerned for her welfare. He'd assumed that the fainting may be due to lack of sleep, food or liquids, combined with the effects of the intense, Mediterranean sun. He also believed it was the effect of her recent heartbreak.

After reassuring him that she felt well again, he went back inside to serve his customers.

Not that long ago, positive energy had pumped through her veins and optimistic thoughts were part of her daily existence. That was before 'death's clutches' snatched her beloved husband.

Death had also stolen some of her dignity and

self-respect.

She was taken unawares by the profile of a woman gazing back at her in the large expansive window of the bar. The image had a haunted look with stooped shoulders and sunken eyes.

She looked away; Incapable of recognising herself as that person. Was that how others perceived her? A broken woman?

Straightening her shoulders and running her fingers through her unruly hair, she glanced again at the reflection. However could she have allowed herself to become the bedraggled person who was staring back at her?

She shook her head several times, before collecting her thoughts.

Reminiscing once more, she reflected on how she'd smelled his cologne before she'd even heard his voice. It suited him so well. Every day since he'd died, she'd generously sprayed his *Eau Savage* cologne onto her skin, to keep the smell of him close to her. She even sprayed it onto her bed linen!

Synchronistically, as if he was confirming her thoughts, he whispered gently in her ear.

"Ma chérie. I want you to continue living your life. Remember what you taught me and the others."

Smiling, she accepted his spiritual presence; knowing that he could be relied upon to turn up at the most opportune moment.

He continued to reassure her.

"You know that I'm always near you."

"I know you're with me. I'll try."

Wiping her cheeks with the back of her hand, she imagined his mischievous smile, reserved especially for her. Pondering on his comment, she allowed herself to relax. She *would* practice what she preached. She thought she *had been* healing herself each day, when she'd visited the labyrinth.

She had! She knew she had!

His familiar smell lingered as he remained close. It was still very early days, but she wondered how long it would take to digest the drastic changes in her life.

Reading her thoughts, he answered.

"It will take as long as it takes. Now go and do what you have to do."

Whilst acknowledging the sincerity of his words, she also allowed herself to admit that she missed his off-the-cuff humour and his abstract manner of encouraging her to deal with things.

Feeling a nuzzle in the nape of her neck, a tender sensation cascaded down the length of her spine; another sign of his spiritual embrace.

Sensing his departure, she felt much better. She bade farewell to Franco and walked around the corner to the patisserie. She hadn't shopped there since Serge's initial diagnosis.

CHAPTER FORTY SEVEN
August

He'd been watching her for a while from the café which was on the opposite side of the road. He'd noticed that she'd been there, at the same time, for the last three weeks. This time, he'd covertly shadowed her around the market stalls, observing her every movement, until she'd finally taken her usual seat on the café terrace.

Watching her grief engulf her, he had wanted to approach her and comfort her. He'd resisted, knowing that it wasn't the right moment to do so.

His curiosity had been fiercely fuelled the last time he'd spoken to her in the café. The probing sleuth in him had enabled him to discover that Suzette had married the much-celebrated sculptor, Serge Couture.

Jurgen had secretly venerated Couture's abstract creations, when he had viewed them in Collioure. He'd admired his other pieces in galleries in America and on the internet.

However, when his latest internet search had alerted him to Serge's death, he'd instantly imagined that he could be the one to console her.

The article had reported that the renowned artist, Couture, had generously bequeathed several of his outstanding creations to the Museum of Modern Art. It also inferred that his legacy would live on with the many other famous artists who'd resided in Collioure in the 1950's and 1960's.

He reflected on the first time he'd seen Suzette and the first time they'd been intimate.

Nostalgia prompted him of the happy times they'd shared; though it didn't prompt him to recall the infuriating times when she'd been stubborn and, try as he might, he'd been unable to control her!

Her previously black hair was now heavily sprinkled with grey and shorter than it used to be.

Initially, he'd been fascinated with her enigmatic, confident persona and her non-conforming habits. Her spiritual wisdom, together with her dry wit, were other quirky characteristics which had been instrumental in his pursuance of her.

He glanced over and he thought she'd seen him. Momentarily, she'd lifted her head from the pages of an English copy of Vogue; her vacant gaze revealing the nothingness around her.

He didn't have the courage to interrupt her from her private rumination. He'd leave it until the next time he saw her. Maybe he'd be able to woo her and she'd be willing to take a chance with him again. He could but hope. He'd bide his time for the right moment.

She stood up to leave and he quickly raised his newspaper to conceal his face. Oblivious to his presence, or anyone else's, she strolled past him.
In his subconscious, he blissfully imagined them together again and smiled.

"I wouldn't be cruel with you this time. I'd be faithful to you, if you'd only give me another chance. We could have such a wonderful life."

Foolish as he was to think that it would, or could happen, fate had already guaranteed that it would never, ever happen. Jurgen had only ever been her *reason* and her *season*. Fortunately, for Suzette, destiny had never intended for him to be her *lifetime*!

His thoughts were interrupted as the trusty testosterone pumped through his veins and stirred his loins. A young, blonde-haired girl sashayed past him. Squeezed into a close-fitting, see-through tee shirt and tight jeans, he was unable to resist, as he ogled her nubile frame.

"Phew. She's a stunner!"

Defending his actions, he exempted himself.

"It's my prerogative to admire all beautiful women. I'm an artist. It's natural for me to look."

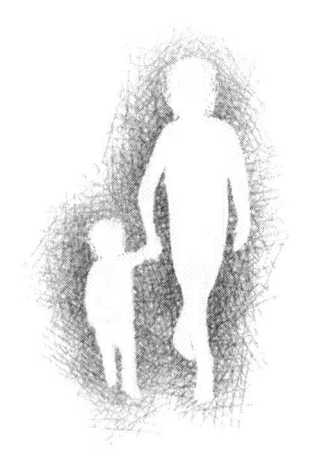

CHAPTER FORTY EIGHT
August

Pleased to see her, Maria gave her a warm smile. The bakery had been in her family for years and had gained a first-class reputation for its bread, delectable cakes and pastries. Suzette had formed a fond friendship with Maria over the years and knew that she would certainly have missed her.

She served her customer and came from behind the serving counter. Embracing Suzette, she held her tightly before speaking.

"Bonjour, mon amie. Comment vas-tu?"

Welcoming the warmness of her embrace, Suzette informed her that she was feeling a little better.

"Bonjour, Maria. Je me sens mieux merci."

Several customers came in and Maria went to

serve them, whilst she perused the rows of temptation displayed in the large chiller cabinet.

Suddenly conscious of the gnawing, hunger pains tugging at her stomach, she waited for the queue to dwindle before approaching the counter to place her order.

She watched as Maria carefully packed a selection of macarons, a large *tarte au citron* and a *tarte aux pommes* into three separate boxes.

After chatting idly with Maria, she placed her purchases into her empty basket and trod the familiar back streets towards her home.

On reaching the sprawling vineyards on the outskirts of the village, she decided to rest for a while on a rickety, wooden bench which was a renowned resting place for the locals.

Sitting quietly, it dawned on her that she'd become oblivious to the beautiful and privileged surroundings in which she inhabited.

Opening the smaller of the three boxes, she lifted out a tiny macaron and took a bite. As the light, airy meringue melted on her tongue, she also detected a slight hint of almond mixed in with the froth of the strawberry-cream filling. Placing the remainder of the macaron into her mouth, she repeated the savouring procedure, slowly enjoying the sensation, before chewing on the crispy shell and swallowing it. It tasted good! Her sleeping taste buds had suddenly come alive!

Self-confessing, she admitted her recent, unhealthy relationship with food, was purely eating miniscule amounts of food just to exist.

Allowing the sun's rays to soothe her, she thought of how Hugo and Sarah had insisted on her eating dinner with them each evening. She'd only shifted the food around the plate; eating just enough to satisfy their fears about her health. Her waning appetite had not disturbed her. Food was of no interest to her. It'd had no taste or appeal, whatsoever!

After witnessing her once-voluptuous figure reduced to the unenviable size of a nubile, catwalk model, she knew that they were keeping a close eye on her mental well-being and physical health.

She hadn't been aware of the deep hollow contours in her cheeks, nor of the dark shadows around her doleful eyes, until she had glimpsed herself in the glass window in the bar. No wonder they were concerned. So were her children, who'd telephoned her on a daily basis to check up on her.

Every evening, following dinner, Hugo and Sarah would accompany her back to her home. Nico would hold tightly onto her hand, walking closely as if he were her bodyguard.

For the first two weeks following Serge's death, Nico had lived with her, sleeping at her side; never leaving her alone. Despite his young age, his parents had informed him from the start about his **grand-père's** illness and explained the process of life and death when Serge had died. They felt that it was important for him to be told the truth about such things.

Ruminating further, she allowed herself to ponder again on the idyllic times she'd shared with her husband. She clearly visualised them tending to their gardens, preparing meals together and avidly discussing the concept of universal law.

On the tough days when she didn't have the strength to face the future, Serge was with her, forever nudging her forward; encouraging her to confront her fears and cherish the life she'd chosen.

The juxtaposed infusion of happiness when he visited her and the sadness she endured when he left, would comfort her and wound her at the same time.

With each spiritual visit, she'd promise him that she'd continue living instead of just surviving. Each time she meant it. Each time she knew that she was only existing!

Automaticity had kicked in after his funeral. She'd functioned robotically; cleaning, gardening, writing in her journal, sitting amongst his tools in his studio and meditating in the clearing.

"Bonjour, Madame."

She was released herself from her private thoughts by a young man walking his dog.

"Bonjour Monsieur."

Gazing down at the empty box on her lap, she had no recollection of eating the six macarons; except perhaps for the very first one, which had transported her into her contemplative state.

Folding the lid on the empty box, she placed it

into her basket on top of the others. Her mood, now lifted, she chuckled to herself.

Rising from the bench, a slightly renewed sense of energy filtered through her body and, as she meandered along the winding country road back towards her home, she felt different.

Although the uncertainty of her life without him in it, brought a fear which infiltrated every inch of her being, intuitively, she knew that she had to keep moving forward.

CHAPTER FORTY NINE
October

Her innate propensity for solitude had, in the past, always brought her healing and today, there was a distinct difference in her mood. The clearing was filled with the subtle sounds of nature. Yet it was somehow noiseless too.

Diligently, she engaged in her daily meditative routine; not necessarily to escape her heartache - she knew that wasn't in the equation - but to open her up to it, address it and accept her life as it was happening.

After traversing the path from the centre of the labyrinth, she reached the summer house and glanced over at the oscillating triangles, stirring gently in the breeze. It was as if they were in sync with her state of being; comforting her, confirming the restoring of her equilibrium.

On recent occasions, the red, yellow and white triangles had oscillated frantically, validating the unbalance that was present in her life.

A calmness surrounded her as she entered the summer house. Opening the wooden, storage box containing her writing tools, she took out some drawing paper, pencils and crayons and set them on the table.

Her wrist moved frenziedly as she sketched coloured images and, annotating each one with phrases and idioms. The mere act of releasing her thoughts onto the sheets of paper, seemed to unblock her negative energies.

One drawing was of several laughing children playing. Their arms were outstretched and they looked as if they were dancing and holding hands.

Above them, she'd drawn an image of a sun which was emerging from behind a cloud. Beneath the image of the children she'd sketched an image of a heart and the number seven.

She stopped sketching for a moment, closely analysing the drawing. Seven children featured in the sketch. The way in which they were reaching out to each other and holding hands, suggested a closeness and a love for each other.

There were seven trees in the background.

It had been seven weeks since Serge had died.

The colour green, of the trees, is related to the heart chakra, which is also associated with psychic healing, love and compassion towards others. The sketch of the heart was also significant.

The purple auras around the children, relating to transformational healing were also noteworthy. She thought of how purple is related to the crown chakra and deduced that her spirit was speaking to her.

She left the drawing on the table and walked outside. The late morning sun was filtering its way through the gaps in the trees and she could hear the water trickling down the side of the triangular sculpture in the centre of the labyrinth. Everything was calm.

Returning inside, she sat down. She knew, from a numerology perspective, that the number seven is deemed to be a spiritual and a sensitive number.

The meaningful relationship between all of the images, which she'd included in the drawing, was slowly unfolding. Accepting that synchronicity had called on her once more to deliver a message, she allowed the drawing of the children with their outstretched arms to reveal the connection.

Her heart was gently nudging her to fulfil her birth mission, by supporting the children again.

She placed her writing tools back into the storage box and gathered up her sketches.

Walking back along the curved, meditation path towards the house, she plucked some herbs which were growing organically amongst the other plants. She'd use them with the fresh fillet of fish that Sarah had brought over for her.

Incremental differences had transpired since Serge's passing. Her temperament and her sleeping habits had fluctuated. Recently, she'd become aware of her innate strength returning and she felt more ready to push on with her life.

Shedding tears had been a regular occurrence for her. She only needed to do something which they'd done together, and the memories would come flooding back.

She'd accepted earlier on in her life that she was an emotional being; one who wasn't afraid to reveal her feelings. She was content with how she was, respecting that others may not react in the same way.

She hadn't been afraid to love either and she'd shared her love with her children, her family, her friends and her partners; latterly Serge.

****

After eating lunch, she decided to take a leisurely meander along the isolated country paths and took a short cut through the overgrown landscape just above the Canal du Midi.

Before attempting the undulating hillsides, which encircled her house, she stopped for a while to inhale the vivid smell of the earth and the clear mountain air.

Determined as she was, to make the climb, she managed to slip several times on the way up, grazing her hands on the dry, gravelled hillside. Her palms were bleeding and the cut on her recently injured finger had reopened.

Retrieving a clean tissue from her pocket, she attempted to wipe the granules of dirt and grit from her wounds.

Sitting down on the rough grass, she caught her breath. Hill walking wasn't usually part of her fitness regime; she much preferred walking on flat ground.

As she gazed across the horizon and down into the valley, she was conscious of the pale blue clouds drifting overhead and the blurred peaks of the Pyrenees in the distance. Mesmerised by the sheer magnificence of the sprawling landscape, the ancient rows of vines and abundant plant life also appeared to be surrounded by a hazy glow.

She'd learnt a long time ago to listen to the silence around her. It was still, except for a small, twittering bird in the nearby bushes, which seemed to be serenading her.

Interconnected with nature, she knew that by just being there, would provide her with some necessary healing.

The place where she was sitting was near to the same piece of shrubland where she'd sat many years ago. She'd been holidaying in Olvano and had wandered off the beaten track.

An eccentric, hippie-type Englishman had been out walking with his dog and he'd escorted her back through the thickly-wooded area to her holiday home. How grateful she'd been at the time. She laughed as she thought of the song, 'Lost in France'. She'd heard a few years ago that he'd died, after being involved in a traffic accident.

She pondered on what her life would have been like if she'd stayed in England and imagined it would've been so very different to the life she'd lived here in France.

After years of longing to live in a different country, she'd manifested her dream when she'd moved to Lezignan. Meeting and marrying Serge had changed her life completely.

Unpredictably, it had changed again.

Reflecting on how she'd navigated her life's unexpected challenges, she was satisfied with how she'd learnt to ride and survive those gravitational tides, which had unexpectedly moved in and out of her life. Those tides had brought with them illness, pain and sorrow; but they'd also brought happiness and contented love.

The spiritual experiences and wisdom she'd gained had been shared with others. She'd used her respectful awareness, to influence and inspire many individuals into making positive shifts in their lives.

Having successfully rode those tidal forces before, she was intuitively aware that her soul would have to surf even more unlived experiences.

She'd deal with whatever was in front of her.

Looking outwards towards the Pyrenees, she began to drift easily into a relaxed state.

In her mind's eye, she was guided to a scene where a little boy was playing ball with his mother in the garden. In another scene, a two year old boy was seated on the back of his mother's bike, as she pedalled through the country lanes, laughing and chatting.

Fully immersed now in her self-regression, she recognised that they were the spirits of herself and Nico. It was yet another confirmation of the message that Serge had given her; her grandson *had* been her son in that previous lifetime.

Throughout her life, her abstract reasoning and symbolic insights were deemed as something odd by others. She'd never questioned her visions and messages; she always accepted what was given to her.

Bringing herself out of her meditative state, her resolve to find herself again was stronger. Her mind was open to new beginnings. She knew it was still too soon to tell how things would pan out, but she'd already embarked on methods to control her energy-depleting thoughts. Nico's daily drop-ins and his persistence in encouraging her to go back to her volunteering role in school, would help to fill the void in her life and give her a renewed sense of purpose. The earlier messages, gleaned from her sketches and the occasional glimpses of the school children as adolescents, that she'd been presented with whilst meditating, had further strengthened her resolve to help them to grow into confident adults.

On her was down the hilly slopes, she felt a hand gently caressing her cheek. She knew it was him.

He stayed alongside her as she tentatively navigated the jutting stones and narrow ledges; not wanting her to fall again.

"Be careful, ma chérie", he whispered.

"I will."

Lighter in spirit now, following her episodes of uncertainty, she felt that she may just be able to face the world again and make peace with her pain.

She knew there'd be occasions when her grief would totally overwhelm her, but she'd deal with it in her own way. For now, she'd try to concentrate on embracing the joys she had in her life and push through her mental torment.

****

The sun was slowly disappearing below the horizon when she went to sit outside on the kitchen terrace. Aware that the mosquitoes would pay her a visit, she lit three large citronella candles and placed two on the table and one on the floor beside her feet. Before going outside she'd also smothered herself in her homemade concoction of mosquito repellent, consisting of equal measures of lavender, lemongrass and rosemary oils blended together with ten parts of liquid witch hazel.

As the timed lights switched on, near the pebbled stream, her eyes followed the expanse of trees, plants and shrubs on the edge of the courtyard in front of her. He'd strategically placed the lights, so that they could still enjoy their garden, even when it was dark.

Cupping her hands around her mug, she slowly sipped the hot, freshly-brewed peppermint infusion. Whilst it quenched her thirst, it did not quench her yearning for the man who usually sat beside her. Missing him was an understatement.

Serge had left and Saudade* had taken his place at the table.

Stepping off the terrace, she strolled over towards the reclining bench which he'd sculpted for her and sat down.

Staring over at his studio, she imagined that she could hear him chipping away at the marble. She'd only checked that it was locked an hour earlier, but with her most precious memories stored inside, she felt an uncontrollable urge to check it again.

*Saudade is an expression used to describe the presence of absence.

On reaching the studio entrance, she placed her outstretched palm on the door, leaned against it for a few minutes and then pressed down on the handle. She was satisfied. It was locked.

When she reached the kitchen terrace, she glanced back at the studio, half expecting him to be following her.

She blew out the candles and stepping inside, contemplated on how she'd appreciated every single moment of the time she'd had him in her life.

Whilst lying in bed, her mind wandered to the school children, learning how to cope with their own differences.

Her intuitive heart knew that her recent decision to return to her volunteering role would be the right one. She needed them, just as much as they needed her.

Subconsciously, she understood that she'd have to step back onto her path and fulfil the purpose that she'd come on earth to fulfil.

She flicked off the light switch and just lay there, in the darkness of the room, evaluating her fluctuating emotions.

How was it, that on some days she felt strong and, on other days when songs, words and smells triggered vivid memories, she'd feel weak?

As she drifted off to sleep, she felt a light sensation on her lips. He'd come to visit her again.

CHAPTER FIFTY
November

She still didn't feel any better. The uncontrollable shivering and the feverish temperature didn't seem to be improving. The flu, which had held her in its stronghold, had kept her captive for the last ten days.

Sarah had been over to see her each day and had left her some medication and food in the kitchen. Suzette didn't want her to come too close to her, in case she caught it and passed it on to Hugo and Nico.

Her legs were unsteady as she stood up. She stumbled and managed to grab hold of the bedside table. Steadying herself, she collapsed onto the bed, exhausted. She felt nauseous and wondered if she'd make it to the bathroom. Her head was throbbing.

Without warning, her breathing altered and she quickly began to hyperventilate. Panicking, she grabbed the phone from the bedside table and rang Hugo's number, praying that he hadn't left for work.

As she heard his phone ringing, the intense shivering returned and she pulled the duvet around her tightly.

"Please answer. Please answer."

She was in luck.

"Hugo. Please come over now. I'm not very well."

Her slurred speech alarmed him.

"I'm coming now. Be with you soon."

The shivering continued and she felt dizzy. The room was spinning around her as she tried to focus on controlling her rapid breathing.

In the final throes of losing consciousness, she hadn't heard him enter the room.

The moment he saw her incoherent and confused state, he knew it was serious.

He hastily pressed the emergency number into his phone and asked for an ambulance to attend urgently. Not knowing what else to do, he sat at the side of her bed, held her hand and waited.

Hearing the ambulance speeding up the drive, he ran downstairs to let them in.

A crew of three paramedics entered the bedroom and immediately started to diagnose her symptoms.

They quickly inserted a canula into her arm. Dehydrated, her blood pressure was dropping to a dangerously low level and her oxygen levels were low. They removed a blood sample from her arm and, after several futile attempts at communicating with her, they lifted her onto a stretcher and carried her downstairs. Carefully placing her into the ambulance, they sped off at high speed, with blue lights flashing and sirens sounding. It was imperative that they reached the hospital, before it was too late.

Hugo rang Sarah and then he followed the ambulance in his car.

Frantic, he rushed into the emergency unit and enquired about Suzette. A nurse guided him into a private waiting room

"Just take a seat here. The doctors are with her now. I'll let you know when you can go in."

As several medical staff rushed in and out of a nearby cubicle, a nurse took Sarah and Nico into the room where Hugo was bent over, nursing his head within his hands. Probing questions were asked and Sarah informed the nurse, that whilst she wasn't her next of kin, she was her niece.

"We thought it was flu. She's been ill for about ten days. She was adamant that she didn't want me to call her doctor."

"Had she been ill prior to that?"

"She'd complained of some throbbing up her arm and tingling in her fingers. She'd cut her finger a while ago and thought it had healed. She'd had a fall whilst out climbing and she'd fell onto her hands. She'd told me the wound had opened up again and both hands were grazed. Oh! She also thought she had a chest infection, because she said she found it hard to breathe."

The nurse scribbled the details onto a case sheet.

"Can we see her now?" Hugo asked.

"Not yet. The doctors are with her now. Do you know if she is allergic to any antibiotics or medicines?"

"Yes. I do know she's allergic to penicillin", Sarah replied.

The nurse left with the information and hurried towards the cubicle.

An hour or so had passed before they were allowed to see her. Sarah didn't want to take Nico in, but seeing that he was on the verge of a serious meltdown, she gave into his demands.

Suzette's unresponsive body was wired up to several machines and an intravenous drip was feeding antibiotics and several liquids into her.

A doctor came to speak with them and he sensitively informed them that Suzette had been diagnosed as having bacterial sepsis. The massive infection had led to her having septic shock and that they'd had to induce her into a coma. He told them, in medical terminology so that Nico wouldn't understand, that bacterial sepsis was a potentially life-threatening condition and they were fearful that it might have been left too late.

Sarah couldn't comprehend what she was hearing. He aunt was normally a healthy, fit person and now she was fighting for her life. She began asking the doctor endless questions.

"Is it because she is older, that she has contracted this?

"No, sepsis doesn't discriminate. Anyone can contract it."

"But she has always been healthy and fit."

"If she's been in good health before her illness, then she has a good chance of recovery. However, I suggest you contact her next of kin. We are going to transfer her to the Acute Intensive Care Unit where she'll be continually monitored."

"Can we stay with her?"

"We need to settle her in first. We'll ring you if there is any change. You can come in to see her later. Ask the nurse for the visiting times."

Bewildered with what was going on around him, Nico interrupted.

"I want to stay with Grand-mère. I don't want to go home."

The doctor knelt and spoke with him.

"You can't stay now, but you can come back later."

Partially satisfied with his answer, he tried hard to control his tapping feet, as his tantrum threatened to erupt. He needed an explanation.

"Why can't I stay?"

"Nico. We need to go and get some things for Grand-mère. We'll come back later on", Sarah promised.

As they watched her being wheeled out of the cubicle and into the lift, being kept alive with the aid of a life-support machine, Hugo wondered why he hadn't noticed how ill she was the day before, when he'd called in to see her.

Whilst walking back to the car park, Sarah quickly made calls to her cousins in Liverpool and Italy. Sobbing, she told them what had happened.

Hearing the panic in Stephanie's voice, she listened as her cousin told her that she'd book herself on the next plane over to Carcassonne.

Equally, Alex had freaked out. He'd also book himself on the next plane over and let her know of his arrival time.

When they reached home, Hugo rang Eve and Gabriel and they immediately rushed over.

"How has this happened?" asked Gabriel.

"Suzette thought she had flu and had taken to her bed to try and recover from it. She didn't want us to send for her doctor. She thought she'd be alright. She didn't want to take antibiotics. The hospital has told us that she has bacterial sepsis and she's now in an induced coma."

He pressed the hospital number on his phone and waited for someone to answer.

"I've diagnosed several patients who have contracted sepsis through open wounds. If only she'd seen her doctor earlier, it could have been prevented."

Fortunately, his friend, who was a doctor in

the Acute Intensive Care Unit, answered his call and Gabriel asked endless questions.

He clicked the 'off' button on his phone.

"She's being constantly monitored and she can have visitors later. They have a flexible visiting policy, but you need to telephone before going. Only close relatives and friends are allowed in and only two visitors at a time at her bedside."

"Has Alex and Stephanie been informed?"

"Yes. I've just rang them. They're booking on the next available flights."

CHAPTER FIFTY ONE
November

As soon as the plane touched down on the runway, Alex grabbed his bag and rushed down the steps and hurried through passport control to where Sarah was waiting.

Hugging her, he began questioning.

"Hi Sarah. How is she? How bad is it? Tell me all about it? Who's with her now."

"Hi. She's still in an induced coma. It was such a shock. She thought she had flu."

His voice quivered, as he continued with his incessant questioning.

"What time's Steph due to arrive?"

"In about three quarters of an hour. Let's go and have a drink whilst we're waiting for her."

They walked upstairs to the restaurant which

overlooked the runway. From where they were sitting, they'd be able to see her plane arriving.

His bloodshot eyes and his shaking hands revealed his torment. He wanted Sarah to go over all the details, even though she'd already told him everything in a previous telephone conversation.

After an impatient wait, they were relieved to hear the roaring of the plane's engine, before they saw it land awkwardly on the short runway.

Seeing Stephanie coming down the steps, they hurried along to passport control to meet her.

As she caught sight of her brother, she gasped. His crumpled face revealed his innermost fears. She knew him well! Her eyes were bloodshot too. Whilst on the plane, her troubled mind had been trying to contain the silent screaming that was begging to be set free. She'd used her scarf to mask the sobbing sounds, as she finally gave in to its pleading.

Luckily, the seats next to her had been empty.

As he saw her blotchy face and puffy eyelids, he knew that she too had been unable to hold it together.

She ran into his outstretched arms. Wrapping his arms around her tiny frame, he held her close. He'd always been very protective of his baby sister.

Once the first involuntary tears had escaped, there was no stopping them. Not caring who was watching them, they allowed them to flow.

Most of the travellers had passed through the airport arrivals area, but some stopped to stare as their initial muffled emotions turned into heavy, uneven sobs.

Alex remembered how his mum had reassured him, by explaining that crying didn't make him any less of a man; it was a natural bodily function and a necessary emotional release.

Stephanie was also comfortable with shedding tears.

He could feel the heaving of her chest as she panted uncontrollably in between sobs, trying to catch her breath.

Sniffing, whilst trying to hold back her own emotions, Sarah handed them some tissues, before stepping back to allow them to comfort each other.

Stephanie began to hyperventilate and her breathing quickened. As her asthma took control, the lump in her throat, knotted and threatened to cut off her airways, her chest muscles tightened and she quickly reached into her pocket for her inhaler.

Bending her head back slightly, she shook the inhaler and placed her lips around it tightly, before releasing two puffs into the back of her throat.

They watched anxiously as she held her breath before slowly breathing out.

Alex had seen her like this many times when she was younger, especially when she became anxious.

Guiding her to a seat, he sat her down and put his arm around her shoulder.

"Are you ok now, Sis?"

"Just let me get my breath back and I'll be ok."

Sarah sat at the other side of her and leaned in against her.

"Sorry, Sarah. How rude of me. I haven't even said hello to you. How is she?"

"It's ok. Hello Steph?"

After sensitively updating her on her mother's illness, Stephanie stood up.

"Can we go now? I need to see her."

CHAPTER FIFTY TWO
November

Even though they were expecting her to be wired up to a life-saving machine, they were still visibly shaken as they saw her lying motionless in the hospital bed.

Hugo and Nico were by her side and Sarah signalled to Hugo to take their son out of the room. Alex and Stephanie needed some time alone with their mother.

Unusually, this time Nico didn't succumb to a meltdown. He allowed his father to lead him out and into a side room.

Sitting on chairs at either side of the bed, they both clasped her hands and watched for any movement.

Alex recalled how she'd played games with

them both when they were little and how she'd made up her own stories and encouraged them to add their own bits. He remembered how she'd taught them manners and how she'd insisted on them being polite and kind to others.

Stephanie remembered how they'd go for long walks in the countryside together and how they'd have girly shopping trips together.

She heard her brother whispering under his breath and the tears trickled down her cheeks.

"Please don't take her now, God. Not yet! How could this be happening so soon after Serge had died? We can't lose you, Mum."

They turned around as they heard the door opening and saw Sarah.

"Can we come back in?"

Considering the ominous circumstances, the doctor had given permission for them all to stay in her room.

Deeply affected by her illness, her family and close friends had felt utterly powerless as they stressfully watched her for movement.

Fifteen minutes later, a male doctor and two nurses entered the room.

Alex introduced himself and his sister.

In her minimally conscious state, Suzette had heard her children sobbing and listened to the doctor explaining the seriousness of her condition. She also heard him say that he'd try to slowly awake her from the coma; but if he switched off the life-support, there was a chance that she'd have difficulty breathing on her own. He was fully prepared to reconnect her again if there was no response.

With much trepidation, they watched as the switches on the life-support machine were turned off, one by one.

As the doctor took hold of her hand and rubbed it, she slowly opened her eyes.

It gave them some hope to see her awake.

Bemused to find herself in a hospital bed with her family around her, her lips curled into a half-smile, before closing her eyes again.

Monitoring her flickering eye movements, the doctor waited and looked for other signs of response.

As she opened her eyes again, sighs of relief filled the room.

"Squeeze my hand, Suzette."

There was movement. Her fingers closed around his hand and her eyelids slowly drooped again.

Weak and agitated, she faintly heard her daughter and son calling out 'Mum' repeatedly.

In her subconscious, she knew that she'd been seriously ill and sensed that her prayerful family were desperately willing her to live. Yet, she had a strange feeling that she was existing in two separate realms.

Gracefully accepting of what was ahead of her, her weightless spirit floated effortlessly as she drifted towards the entrance of a tunnel.

She watched, in wonder, as Serge's blurred image approached her. She could never resist that alluring smile; the one he kept just for her.

With her arm outstretched, she waited for her husband to take her with him.

She could feel a hand, but it wasn't his.

Sitting near her, Nico had grabbed hold of her hand and was holding it close to his chest. He'd also been observing the frantic, flickering lines on the machine and sensed unease.

His earlier, incessant questioning had irked one of the senior nurses, who thought that it was very inappropriate for a small child to be interested in the life-monitoring device, or in death.

His daily visits to her bedside had resulted in him acting in an even stranger manner than was usual for him. He'd repeatedly called her 'Maman', saying that he was sorry and that he'd never leave her again.

Mystified as to why he was saying those things, Hugo and Sarah had tried to console him.

He'd refused to answer their questions and had repetitively patted his fingers on the bed and tapped his feet on the tiled floor.

Suzette's mind flipped through segments of time. She'd never quite grasped the concept of it; forever wanting it to remain still, so that she could embrace every moment of the joyful events.

She experienced visions of herself as a little girl, playing in the garden. She could see herself as a teenage rebel and a youthful, happily-married woman with two children. Later, graphic images of herself as a struggling, single mother flashed up before her eyes and then she saw herself as a middle-aged woman in various professional roles. Her dear friend, Dolly, hovered in front of her, with that knowing smile. The images of her mother and father, along with deceased relatives and friends kept on coming, whooshing past her now.

She re-lived a scene of when she was ten years old. She had seen faces in the curtains in her bedroom and she'd had dialogues with 'a presence' in the room when she was alone. When she'd voiced what she'd seen, she was told she was a daydreamer. That was the time she knew she'd follow her own path and not the one that others expected of her. Unknowingly, at the time, she'd started the process of connecting with herself and her life journey had since been filled with many learning experiences.

Bathing in the otherworldly tranquility, she watched, in amazement, as even more brightly-coloured images of her life flowed past her. Brief flashes of the many people who'd questioned her philosophical views, labelling her a fantasist, an oddity, a recluse, skimmed past her.

Initially, when younger, their comments had hurt her. As she'd got older, they didn't faze her as much. Next, she saw herself with Serge in spirit form, making a pact to 'awaken' together before reincarnating.

The images disappeared and, in a flash, she

came face to face with him. Wanting to embrace him, she reached out once again.

"Grand-mère. What do you want?"

Slowly opening her eyes, she struggled to focus on his features.

"He's waiting for me. I have to go now."

"Who is waiting for you Grand-mère?"

"Grand-père is waiting for me."

"Is he? Can I come with you, Grand-mère? I want to see him too."

She smiled. Her grandson had enriched her life. He'd also enriched many others' lives and he'd continue to do so. He'd fulfil his birth mission and follow his own path; making people more aware of the importance of being 'of service' to others and of not being judgemental.

"Not this time, darling. I'll come back and visit you."

"Like Grand-mère Nicole and Grand-père?"

She didn't reply. How could she answer him?

The intense allure of finally being reunited with Serge was steadily weakening.

From a leaning position, he quickly climbed onto the bed and snuggled into her limp body. The nurses, who'd previously stopped him from sitting on the bed, acknowledged his urgent need and disregarded the hospital rules.

Spluttering, Hugo didn't attempt to obstruct him either. The circumstance was reminiscent of the time he'd also laid beside his own maman, as she took her last breath.

Nico's young mind was accepting of death in a grown-up way. When Serge had died, he'd shown great courage. Unsurprisingly, his disposition was equally resilient as he lay beside her. He wasn't going to let her leave him; not yet.

She closed her eyes once more. He was standing in front of her, surrounded by a large cluster of white luminous orbs.

The tunnel reminded her of an unforeseen accident, which had occurred on a country road in Lezignan, just before she'd met Serge. She'd been drawn into a similar tunnel and remembered the blissful feeling and the comforting light. It was as if she was being gently wrapped in a blanket of love. She'd been disappointed then, when an invisible thread had pulled her back into her human form.

This time, irresistibly attracted to the light, she was almost there again. She removed her hand from Nico's clutch, lifted her outstretched arm and waited.

His grip strong, he grabbed hold of it again and wouldn't let go. She could feel the trembling warmth of his body against hers as he whispered in her ear.

"No, Grand-mère. Do not go."

Opening her eyes again, she saw his forlorn face. How could she even think of leaving him?

Her family stood around her bed, anxiously waiting, hoping, praying.

Her heart was subtly whispering to her and she closed her eyes again. Knowing that he'd fully understand, she delivered her decision.

"Serge, I can't be with you yet. I can't leave our little boy."

Nico's grip tightened.

"I'm afraid you're going to have to wait for me a while longer, darling."

He bowed his head slightly.

"I understand, ma chérie. I'll wait for you."

She leant over to kiss him.

Barely touching her lips, he held back from totally embracing her. If he held onto her for too long, she'd want to stay with him. Moreover, he wouldn't want to let her go back.

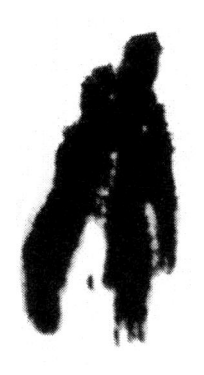

Yet, both understood that her time on earth wasn't finished. She'd more work to do.

Like once before, the invisible thread pulled her steadily backwards, away from the tunnel, steering her spirit back to inhabit its human form.

Using his sixth sense, Nico had witnessed their conversation.

"Père. Grand-mère is coming back to us. She was going to see Grand-père in a white tunnel. I saw him, honestly. She is not going now."

A warm, loving energy surrounded them. In awe of this seven year old boy's vision, they all stood and waited; hoping against hope that their prayers had been answered.

She opened her eyes again. It seemed that at one moment, she'd taken her last breath and the next minute, she was conscious.

The medical team were at the ready, to resuscitate. There was no need. The levels on the machinery at the side of her bed were registering normal.

Witnessing another near-death experience had been surreal for Suzette. As she gazed into the little boy's eyes, she could feel that instantaneous soul connection.

Fate had fetched her to what she thought was the final place in her life, but her soul had spoken with her free will and an important decision had been made.

She sensed that her love for her grandson was only one of the purposes for her return. She'd always experienced strong déjà vu feelings when she was with him.

Her cherished family, her dearest friends and the schoolchildren were the other reasons.

More pages of her life would need to be written and Nico Serge Couture would be there to help her write them.

He'd teach her far more than she could ever teach him!

No, it wasn't her time to go, yet!

SUSAN M HIGGINS

UNEXPECTED VISITS

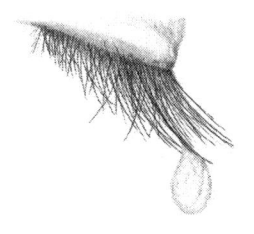

On occasions when I least expect
I hear a song
It brings back memories
Of happy times
Sometimes sad

On occasions when I least expect
A word is whispered
I smell you near me
I feel your touch
It comforts me

On occasions when I least expect
Nostalgia flows
Out of my eyes and falls
Down my cheeks
Sometimes gently, sometimes not

Susan M Higgins 2020 ©

About the author

Susan Higgins is a semi-retired teacher of English, a fictional/technical author and an experienced facilitator of change.

As an author of fiction, her writing is inspired by the Languedoc region of France and her perpetual passion for her own self-development and the advancement of others; on both an academic and a spiritual level.

Over the past ten years, she has designed and delivered creative writing courses. She has also written and delivered numerous self-development programmes.

As an author of non-fiction, her written matter includes technical procedures and media journals for various reputable organisations.

Thank you for choosing my book.
If you enjoyed reading it,
I'd be most grateful if
you would leave a review
on amazon.co.uk

Printed in Poland
by Amazon Fulfillment
Poland Sp. z o.o., Wrocław